Let us hear the conclusion of the whole ma
Fear God, and keep his commandments: for th
is the whole duty of man.

MARONE MEMOIRS

MARONE MEMOIRS

An immigrant story

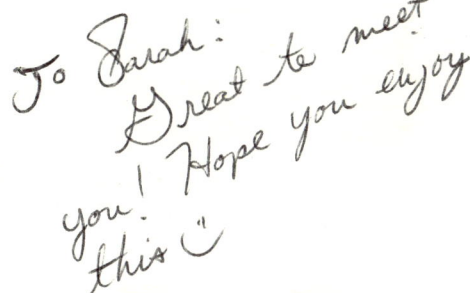

Sarah E. Lingley

Cover image: The village of Laurenzana, Italy.
Photo courtesy of James Marone Hopkins.

Copyright © 2003 by Sarah E. Lingley.

Library of Congress Number: 2003096069
ISBN :   Hardcover   1-4134-2835-5
                  Softcover   1-4134-2834-7

All rights reserved. No part of this book may be reproduced or transmitted in any form or by any means, electronic or mechanical, including photocopying, recording, or by any information storage and retrieval system, without permission in writing from the copyright owner.

This book was printed in the United States of America.

To order additional copies of this book, contact:
Xlibris Corporation
1-888-795-4274
www.Xlibris.com
Orders@Xlibris.com
20204

CONTENTS

Acknowledgements 9
Preface 11
Introduction 13
Chapter One
    If You Want . . . Yes, You May 19
Chapter Two
    Life Together 23
Chapter Three
    . . . Life Apart 27
Chapter Four
    Wheat Harvest 29
Chapter Five
    Family 31
Chapter Six
    Extended Visit 36
Chapter Seven
    Trouble 39
Chapter Eight
    Forty-day Wait 42
Chapter Nine
    Remedy 45
Chapter Ten
    The Unexpected 50
Chapter Eleven
    Old Country Behind, New Country Ahead 57
Chapter Twelve
    Assistance Needed 62
Chapter Thirteen
    Stranded 68

Chapter Fourteen
    Farewell, Prinzess Irene 73
Chapter Fifteen
    Hello, Prinz Friedrich Wilhelm 76
Chapter Sixteen
    Arrival, Rescue . . . Finally 83
Chapter Seventeen
    How It Happened 89
Chapter Eighteen
    How It Ended 97
Chapter Nineteen
    Life in America 101
Chapter Twenty
    Progress 105
Chapter Twenty-one
    Hello . . . Goodbye 109
Chapter Twenty-two
    The Guest from Hartford 116
Chapter Twenty-three
    Help Wanted 121
Chapter Twenty-four
    Rosa's Not Well 125
Chapter Twenty-five
    Good News . . . Bad News 128
Chapter Twenty-six
    Life Without Grazia 131
Chapter Twenty-seven
    Goodbye, New York 135
Chapter Twenty-eight
    Home . . . Right Where It's Always Been 139
Epilogue 143
Historical Information 153
Family Tree 157
Chronology 158
Author's Note 173

To my great-grandparents, Raffaele and Rosa Pavese Marone, and to each of my relatives, I dedicate this book.

ACKNOWLEDGEMENTS

I am deeply indebted to many individuals for their assistance in the completion of this book. It is my desire to thank everyone, though I am afraid that I will never be able to express my gratitude sufficiently. I would like to extend my deepest thanks:

To my Lord and Savior Jesus Christ, first and foremost, for the guidance and direction that He has given me. Thank You for proving Your faithfulness to me in ways I will never forget. May You be honored through every breath I take, and receive all the glory from the talents and abilities You have given me.

To my parents, Henry and Christine Lingley, for their deep love and support. Mom, you were always there to help me when I was trying to figure out the dates and details. I appreciate your willingness. Dad, you were always there to nudge me in the right direction. Thanks, I love you both.

To my siblings—Heather, Henry, Jeremiah, Esther and Hannah—for their support. Thanks for putting up with me when I was too deep in thought or too focused on this project to be good company (Hope the story is good enough to compensate). You'll never know how much your interests in this project kept me going.

To my brother, Jeremiah Lingley, for his assistance. I honestly don't know where I'd be without your techno-abilities; probably still sitting in front of a broken computer pulling my hair out. You have helped me so much. Thanks for lending so much of your time to help this project run smoothly and come, finally, to such a good end.

To my grandma, Ella Piacentini, for her loving support and pride. Though she died before I was able to complete this book, she stood behind me from the very beginning and was more proud of this book than anyone I know. Her dream had always been to see me get published and I'm only sorry I didn't finish this in time to give her the first copy as I'd planned. Thanks for all those phone calls, hugs and best wishes; I'll love you forever, Grandma.

To my great-aunt, Peggy Lehan, whose memories of bygone days I consulted often. I appreciate your willingness to take the time to share your experiences as a little girl, and what life was like over ninety years ago. Clearly, this book would have been a very difficult project to complete without the information you lent.

To my cousins, James Marone Hopkins (Hope I get to meet you some day) and Armand Maccarone, for their assistance. Your knowledge and experience gained through personal research and individual visits to Italy proved to be the source I consulted most. Thanks for your patience in answering my endless questions. Thanks for sharing my vision; your words of encouragement helped keep me going. I'm going to miss all those emails.

To Amelia Battalino (I love the way you ramble), Donald Battalino, Anna Marone Bredice, Lorraine Hopkins, Chester and Rosanne Kozak, Catherine Lally, Ed Lehan (Thanks for the cassette), Mary Fran Lombardi, Armand Maccarone, Justin and Lucia Maccarone, Ralph Maccarone, Antoinette Marone (Thanks for letting me borrow the snap shot), Frances Marone, Frank and Elsie Mazzarella, Paul Mazzarella, Ralph Mazzarella, Millie Rizzo, Mike Rizzo, Catherine Shaw and Ben and Johanna Snyder. I appreciate the time and effort you took to share your memories; they have made this book more complete than I ever could have done on my own.

To the entire Marone family for their support. I hope you enjoy reading the story of our family.

To the Tim Betts family for their technical assistance.

To my good friends, Amanda Easley and Deborah Diller ("Do I know you?"), for standing on the sidelines cheering me on.

To the many other friends and acquaintances who lent their encouragement and support. Every thought and prayer was felt and appreciated.

PREFACE

History had always been my favorite subject, and that of my ancestors even more so, understandably.

During the summer of 2001, the thought occurred to me that no written record of my ancestors' lives existed. From time to time, a few of my relatives would allude to portions of their childhood or younger days, but to my knowledge, none of that information had ever been documented.

Being as I am, deeply interested in literature, the thought of documenting the records that my family lacked also occurred to me. Thus, in August of 2001, my endeavor to write this book began. By late spring of 2002, I'd gathered enough information, and had done enough research, to begin writing.

In my attempt to put my family history on paper, I have also made a vigorous attempt to keep the words contained in this volume historically accurate. I have strongly relied on the memories of the individuals who experienced the events in this book. They were there, they lived through it all, and they know best what it was like.

It is with much honor that I have labored to complete this book, knowing that there will no longer be an empty space on the shelf when it comes to my family history. Few of my relatives mentioned in this book remain today, but when the last one has gone, their story will live on.

INTRODUCTION

Many years ago, a man and his wife lived in the small hill village of Laurenzana, tucked quietly away in southern Italy. Their names were Antonio and Graziado Marone.

Like most Italians, Antonio and Graziado had been living on the acreage they called home all their lives, acreage that had belonged to his father, his grandfather, his great-grandfather and so on. Their wealthy social status and comfortable life had come from the same source. Antonio and his wife were the largest property owners in Laurenzana, and they grew large crops of wheat and owned many sheep. Antonio leased out portions of his land, including portions of his wheat fields on occasions, and the other villagers benefited from the local supply of wheat and Parmesan cheese.

On February 15, 1867, Antonio and Graziado's first son was born. They named him Raffaele and, while they also had a daughter whom they called Maria Carmella, Raffaele would be the one to carry on the Marone name and who would receive Antonio's possessions later on. For this Antonio and Graziado were pleased, and took great pride in calling Raffaele their son.

* * *

Twelve years later, in a small room above the noisy streets of New York City, lived a man with his wife and their small son, Michele. It was here, on March 2, 1879, when a baby girl was added to the small family. Her parents, Donato and Maria Giovanna Pavese, named her Rosa. They had left their home in Laurenzana, Italy, and relocated to America as immigrants.

Like most immigrants, the Paveses had left behind a better life. They had traded a wealthy social status for tenement life on the streets of New York. The familiarity of family and friends was traded for the strangers who bustled through the streets speaking weird languages. And while the small apartment they called home was all but spacious and lovely, the Paveses had plans to settle down and build a new future.

* * *

Maria Carmella and Raffaele strolled through Laurenzana atop a mule, wearing finery of soft silk and starched white. They lived a relaxed life, one where hired hands and servants tended the daily tasks of the farm and house around them. Growing up in such an environment, Raffaele and Maria Carmella were fashioned into elegant and stylish individuals. The education they received made them all the more socially advanced.

But underneath the finery and fashion, Raffaele longed to become a real man. He quickly tired of watching the hired hands tend his family's property, and he dreaded wasting day after day in the cool shade. Raffaele knew, however, that if he was to get his pure white shirt wrinkled or dirty, or make even the tiniest tear in the soft velvet of his knickers, his mother would go into a rage.

After much inward discontentment, Raffaele finally shared his troubles. To his surprise, neither his parents nor his sister scolded him. Though they did remind him that to leave his wealth and finery behind meant that they would be difficult to find again, should he change his mind in the future. But Raffaele was decided.

* * *

When Rosa was a toddling year and a half old, she joined her mother one day on a short trip of errands. Out in the streets, Maria Giovanna met an acquaintance on Second Avenue and the two women stopped to talk. Rosa stood close by, with her mother's apron string tightly in her hand. When Maria Giovanna finally turned to go, she discovered that Rosa was no longer with her. Maria Giovanna cried out and began searching through the crowd, turning around and around and then weaving in and out among the people.

Soon, Maria Giovanna's acquaintance caught on and the two women ran through the streets. Hours passed and little Rosa was still nowhere to be found. The two women finally parted and went their separate ways toward home. When Donato returned from work, Maria Giovanna greeted him with sobs. Donato listened as his wife poured out the entire story. They took Michele to a friend's house and went directly to the police, later notifying newspaper companies and all of their friends.

Weeks passed, and the Paveses continued to look for Rosa. One day they got wind of a baby being held by a wealthy couple somewhere in "The Bronx." Donato and his wife hurried there, hoping that the baby was Rosa. When they found the apartment, they could hear a baby crying. The police was notified, and the Paveses waited out in the street until deputies arrived. Emotions were a mix of fear, nervousness, and excitement. The police finally arrived and entered the house. After a few minutes, the crying stopped and a policeman came outside carrying a baby in his arms.

It was Rosa. Donato and Maria Giovanna ran to grab her. The policeman said that he and his men had found the baby under a bed among lots of toys. Donato thanked the officer, but as the Paveses turned to go, a man opened a window from the house Rosa had been taken from. "My wife and I don't have any children," he yelled, "so we'd like to adopt. Won't you take money for the child? We'll give you any amount, just name it." The Paveses turned away without a second thought.

Shortly after, Donato decided to send Maria Giovanna and their two children back to Laurenzana. There they would be safer, and free from further threats of kidnapping. Donato bought tickets for them as soon as he could, then saw them off at the dock. As they slowly drifted away, he swore that Rosa would never again set foot on American soil.

* * *

In 1884, Raffaele Marone said goodbye to his family and village. He left the surroundings of Laurenzana and headed to America by boat. Once there, he got a job, working as a laborer in a cotton mill. His job provided the necessary funds to keep himself clothed, fed and housed. He shared a rent in Framingham, New York.

Still in New York a year later, Raffaele decided to become an American citizen. Though he worked hard, life was not easy. Raffaele encountered prejudicial individuals who disliked foreigners. But Raffaele was stubborn, and determined not to let a few bullies ruin his dreams.

Early one morning before work, Raffaele reached towards the fireplace accessories with a mean smile. He chose the poker, and thrust it with determination into the hottest coal until the iron was red hot. Pounding the end into a nasty point, Raffaele hammered until his strong arm ached and his eyes shone with satisfaction. The poker, now transformed into a weapon of defense, was cooled and ready to be hidden away. Raffaele carefully slid the poker up his pant leg and headed to work.

Arriving at the mill, Raffaele nonchalantly busied himself with his duties at the filing bench. Perhaps it was his nonchalant manner that led him to mindlessly bend his leg, driving his pant cuff upwards and revealing his hidden weapon of defense.

A co-worker noticed, and let out a yell. "He's got a poker up his pants!"

Though news of Raffaele's weapon had soon reached every ear in the factory, no one seemed to bother him. Until he left for home. Waiting for him outside the door, the other mill workers had formed a gang against Raffaele. Unbeknown to any of them, however, the foreman of the mill had heard of the contention, and he walked out the door just as the men were preparing to begin their fight.

At a time when no one else had anything to say, Raffaele was as bold as ever. "Give me your best man, and I'll fight him." A ring began to form among the men, and with fists as hard as his head, Raffaele quickly proved that he was a man through and through.

In addition to making a name for himself, Raffaele developed a liking for boxing and later tried his fists at a few amateur events.

He also joined a political group, where he became a member of the Democratic Party and often hung out at the Party clubhouse on Second Avenue. Now a full-fledged Italian American, Raffaele was even given a nickname, "Rockefeller."

* * *

When Maria Giovanna returned with Michele and Rosa, the villagers of Laurenzana were very understanding. The topic of Rosa's kidnapping, however, quickly disappeared from the villagers' lips as she and Michele grew. Contrasted against the streets and tenements of New York, their playground was now rolling hills, and their playmates were family and new friends. They were soon enrolled in school, where they began their studies for an education suitable for their class.

It was several years later before Donato finally returned to his family in Laurenzana. In still another location, the Paveses began yet another new life, one that required little physical labor and virtually no work at all. Their clothes were prim and proper and the food hearty and rich.

* * *

As time passed for Raffaele, he began to find the time and finances to make visits back home. His family and friends were glad to see him, and he enjoyed a break from working in the mill. Raffaele's mother approved of the visits, confident that the relaxation was healthy for him. But soon enough, Raffaele would hear the voice from deep inside calling him back to America. So, he would board the next boat and wave goodbye until the next visit.

One such visit took place in 1895. While he had now been traveling between countries for eleven years, this particular visit back to Italy was more than a "routine" journey. There was something weighing heavily on Raffaele's mind, and it was something that would change his life and his future forever. And this is the story . . .

CHAPTER ONE

If You Want . . . Yes, You May

Raffaele casually sipped wine from his glass as he and his father shared a meal. They were sitting at a small table in a low lit corner of a diner, and the room was filled with the low hum of several conversations taking place at once. Their own conversation added to the hum.

Antonio set his own wine glass back on the table and looked at his son. "Well, to be honest with you, Raffaele, I can't say that's a difficult question to answer. You're twenty-eight now, and if you want to get married, then you certainly may." Antonio took a few bites of his dinner, then set his fork down as if a thought had just occurred to him. "Is there anybody in particular whom you're considering?"

"Well, yes. I was thinking about Rosa Pavese; I'm very taken with her."

Antonio raised an eyebrow. "Wait a minute," he said with a chuckle, "you don't mean Donato and Maria Giovanna Pavese, do you?"

"Sure I do," said Raffaele as he set his glass down. "That's the only Rosa Pavese I know. Why do you ask?" He leaned forward and placed his forearms and elbows on the edge of the table. A crust of buttered bread remained on his dish, and he reached for it.

"Come on, Raffaele," Antonio was saying, "don't tell me you've been in America too long to remember the way Donato feels about his daughter."

"Okay, so Donato is particular." Raffaele picked up his glass to take another sip of wine.

19

"Well, I just don't think you'll have much success in getting permission to marry his daughter, that's all. But," said Antonio, moderately lifting his hands. "I'm not going to stop you from confronting him."

A short time later, Raffaele found himself riding a mule towards the Paveses' house. White clouds of hot air snorted from the mule's nostrils as the clip-clopping sounds on the cobblestones echoed through the narrow streets. Raffaele could feel the mule's body heat beneath him as he rode past houses with their windows glowing in the darkness.

The servant girl answered the door at Raffaele's knock, and led him to a nearby chair. She disappeared through a doorway, and Donato Pavese came bustling through a few minutes later.

"*Buona sera**, Raffaele. Welcome to my home, do come in." Donato's wife was close behind him and she smiled her greeting to Raffaele.

Raffaele stood to greet his friends, and the trio walked towards another set of furniture in an adjoining room. At Donato's motion, Raffaele took a seat on a cushioned chair.

"Well, a pleasant evening out there?" Donato asked. The servant girl had gone for some wine, and the men engaged in small talk while they waited.

"Yes, it is. Just that perfect time of the year where it's not too warm or too chilly. And how are things with you lately? I expect you've been rather busy?"

Donato Pavese laughed. "That I have. I feel like I've never been busier before. Of course, now that Michele is pursuing politics and all of that, he's not around much to help me out, you know . . ."

"And how is all that political stuff coming for him?" interjected Raffaele.

"Oh, he drops in now and then to tell me all about it, but well, I'll just say that politics isn't my thing and frankly, I don't understand much of what he talks about."

The men laughed, but were soon calmed as the servant girl entered with a tray. She placed it on a nearby table and picked up the glasses. "Sir Pavese, Sir Marone."

"*Grazie*.*"

The girl curtsied, and left directly, leaving the trio alone once again.

Donato Pavese cleared his throat. "Now, what was it that brought you here tonight?" He sat back more comfortably in his chair and took a sip of his wine.

"Well, Mr. Pavese, Mrs. Pavese, I've actually come to ask your permission about something." Raffaele paused to take a polite sip of his own wine.

"Our permission?" Donato eyed his wife.

"Yes. You see, I really admire your daughter and, if you would allow me to, I would be honored to take her as my wife."

Donato was quiet for a minute. "Raffaele, do you know that you are not the first person to confront me on this issue?"

Surprised, Raffaele shook his head.

"Well, I'll make a long story short. A certain man recently approached me about Rosa and asked me if I would let him marry her. Do you know why I said no?" Donato hurried on without allowing his guest to answer. "This man who came to me was from The Bronx, you know, in New York, USA. Anyhow, there he ran a chocolate factory and, as I understand it, handled quite a business. Anyhow, I knew he greatly adored Rosa, and yet I had to say no." His eyes were studying the wine glass in his hand, but it was clearly evident that his mind was far away. "Raffaele," he continued as he looked up. "I said no to that man because he wouldn't promise to keep Rosa here." His eyes met Raffaele's as if to give an indirect answer to the question of matrimony.

"But, sir, that's just it. I'm not asking you to allow Rosa to come back to America with me. I know a lot of men back there who are working hard and then sending the money back here to their wives and children. If you would allow that scenario to work for me and Rosa, I would be very pleased." Raffaele sat still while Donato comprehended and considered his offer.

"Hmm, that's an interesting proposal," said Donato. He turned to his wife.

Maria Giovanna had nothing to offer except a hesitating glance, and the two sat in silence for, what seemed to Raffaele, an eternity. Raffaele knew there was a lot they needed to think through before saying yes, yet it was a hard wait.

"Yes, I think your suggested scenario would work," Donato finally stated. "Raffaele, you have my permission to marry my daughter."

* *Grazie ('grattzja):* thank you
Buona sera (bwona' sera): good evening

CHAPTER TWO

Life Together . . .

"Now, you need to be pinned right here," said Rosa to herself. She held two pieces of material together as she began to stick pins through them. "There, now that sleeve is ready to be sewn." Rosa was sitting on her bed constructing her wedding gown that she had spent weeks fitting, cutting and pinning. All around her lay different shapes and sizes of the gown material, as well as scissors, pins and thread. She was pinning the collar together when her brother, Michele, popped his head into the bedroom.

"Rosa, dinner's ready. *Madre** asked me to call you." When he noticed that Rosa was at work, Michele entered the room and walked over to the bed. He rested his hand on the corner post as he looked around at the remaining pieces of the gown. His eyes grew big as he whistled. "I don't see how you know where to put all those different pieces."

Laugher escaped Rosa's lips as she picked up a particular piece from several differently shaped ones. "Oh, it's not really that hard. Besides, practice makes perfect and I've had lots of experience in sewing clothes." She lay down her gown and got up. "C'mon, let's go before we miss dinner."

A few weeks later, after much time and effort had been put toward sewing, baking, cooking and planning, Rosa Pavese and Raffaele Marone were married on January 6, 1896. The abundant portions of food, wine and merriment punctuated the occasion with cheer and love of life. Rosa and Raffaele, and all the friends and family who had gathered, would remember the day as a very happy one.

When all the celebrations were finally over, Rosa and Raffaele settled comfortably into their new life. Raffaele was proud of the land and possessions he'd acquired from his father. Both their homes were modest, nicely built brick dwellings that housed them separately in summer and winter.

At their summer home, the Marones enjoyed large wheat fields that spread over the distant hills, and livestock that grazed on the fresh green grass. Goats, housed in a small shed under the backside of the home, provided the Parmesan cheese for the Marones' own use and for sale to locals and foreigners.

Rosa especially loved the summer home, where she spent a lot of time cooking at the big hearth. On either side of the hearth was a large wooden bench stretched out in opposite directions. There was a ceiling-to-floor cabinet nearby which held a portion of the previous year's wheat crop, conveniently stored where local villagers could purchase it. In the center of the room stood a stove for heat, and at the far end was the bedroom which Rosa and Raffaele shared. In addition to the bed and clothes cabinets, there was the chair that Rosa sat in when her hairdresser came at the beginning of each day.

"So, how are things down in the fields?" Rosa asked one afternoon. The months following their wedding had passed quickly, and summer was now in bloom, an open window allowing wisps of her hair to be blown by the breeze.

"Pretty well," said Raffaele as he sat down on one of the wooden benches that protruded from either side of the big hearth. "The wheat appears to be healthy. I was just speaking with one of the men yesterday and he said that the stalks are growing strong." He paused as he watched Rosa add the finishing touches to the meal she was preparing. She moved about the large room with ease. Finally, he added, "I rang the dinner bell, so the men will be coming in any minute now."

"Thank you, dear. This is all finished now, and ready to go on the table." Rosa smiled as she turned to her husband, but he had turned to look out the window and didn't notice her. As if he had tilled the ground with his own hands, and placed the seeds into the dirt one by one, Rosa noticed a certain air of personal gratification as Raffaele glanced out the window and beyond the village houses. She smiled again.

"All ready ma'am?" asked the servant girl, who had just entered the room.

"Yes, it's all ready and waiting. *Grazie.*"

Rosa turned from the completed meal and left the servant girl to carry the platters and bowls to the big table in the next room. Rosa provided the hired hands with a daily lunch that they took to the fields each morning. Each evening, the men enjoyed a hearty meal around the table indoors.

"Well, I'm glad the first crop we are calling our own is coming along so well. It's hard to believe harvest time is almost here." Rosa reached for the two plates prepared for Raffaele and herself, and joined him on the bench. As they began to eat the hot food, the hired men could be heard from the other room. Even though the servant girl was there to tend their needs, Rosa listened with half an ear at their entrance.

"I've been thinking," Raffaele was saying.

Rosa turned her attention from the noises in the other room to her husband's voice. "Mmm-hmm?"

"Well, I've been thinking that I am just about ready to go back to America."

Rosa had known that it would be coming soon. As it was, Raffaele had left America many months ago. "Okay."

"Well, I just thought I'd let you know," said Raffaele. To his surprise, Rosa's response seemed to be just as understanding as his parents', who had always seemed to comprehend his desires to return to America. In the recent months, Raffaele had begun to discover that Rosa Pavese Marone had a very laid-back personality.

*   *   *

"Well, what's her name? Why didn't you bring her back with you? Where did you leave her?" The questions came one after another from Raffaele's co-workers. His return to America as a married man had quickly become the butt of many jokes.

"Her name's Rosa . . ."

"Oh, how nice," interrupted one man in a mimicking tone.

Raffaele eyed him, annoyed by the fake interest. "Her parents didn't want her to come to America," he continued, "so, I left her in Laurenzana." He turned back to his work, uninterested in their questions.

His days filled with hard work, Raffaele received little respite when he returned to the small rented room at the end of each day. The food he managed to obtain was meager compared with rich and hearty Italian food, though somehow Raffaele's love and enjoyment of physical labor weighed far more in value to him. Out of the money he earned, a small portion was taken for his own use and the rest was sent home to Rosa.

Back in Laurenzana, Rosa plunged into her new set of routines with vigor.

* *Madre (mah'dreh):* mother

CHAPTER THREE

. . . Life Apart

"Rosa, what on earth are you doing?" inquired the servant girl one day. She stood aside as Rosa came bustling by with an arm load of items. "Rosa, I asked you a question."

"Yes, I know you did," came a holler through the doorway. A few seconds later, Rosa reappeared. But only momentarily. "I'm moving," she stated, then vanished out of sight. A few minutes later she was back with another arm load.

Finally, the servant girl was too curious to exhibit further patience. Following Rosa, she watched Rosa unload her arms onto the bed. "Okay, so why are you moving everything into this room?" she asked.

"Well," said Rosa, "I decided I didn't want to sleep in that big bed in that big room all alone." She started for the door, and added over her shoulder, "I figured that while Raffaele is gone, I'll just sleep in here."

The servant girl laughed to herself and slowly shook her head. "Suit yourself."

Shortly after Raffaele departed to America, Rosa made a wonderful discovery. "I'm pregnant with our first child," she celebrated to a friend. "Raffaele would be so proud if he knew." Their new baby was expected to arrive early in 1897, but Rosa was too busy to sit and mull in excitement.

"Summer's here and that means wheat harvest. I have so much to do."

"Now Rosa, don't push yourself too hard. Tsk, tsk, you should slow down, dear, and take some time to rest."

"But don't worry, *Madre,*" Rosa insisted, "I'll be leaving for my winter home in a matter of months. I will be able to get all the rest I need then." Though laid-back as she was, Rosa's determination was quick to shine through as she went from one task to another. Soon enough, winter arrived and Rosa found herself celebrating what would have been her and Raffaele's first Christmas, then their first wedding anniversary, and their birthdays. It was only four short days after her own birthday that Rosa celebrated the birth of their first child. Grazia Marone arrived on March 6, 1897. Rosa didn't know it at the time, but Grazia's birth would be the first of many to which Raffaele would not attend.

Grazia grew fast. By the time Rosa returned to the summer home, Grazia fit into the pompous lifestyle well. She and Rosa began to enjoy life together.

"Rosa, where are you?" Maria Giovanna said one day. She stood inside the door of the big room where Rosa could usually be found. The large hearth had a small fire burning, but Rosa wasn't around. "Rosa, Rosa," Maria Giovanna continued to call.

Finally, Rosa bustled in. "I'm sorry, *Madre*, I didn't hear you calling. Oh, I've been so busy . . . what can I do for you?"

"Well, for one thing, here's a letter from Raffaele," offered Maria Giovanna. "Donato picked it up yesterday; and here's a few things for you as well." She began to empty a basket of baked goods onto the nearby table as she spoke.

"I'm so glad that he's back from the fields. I do appreciate his help." Rosa was glad to see an envelope from Raffaele, but she set it aside as she helped her *madre*.

"Oh, he doesn't mind taking the sheep to pasture one bit. Of course, with Raffaele not home you certainly need the help . . ."

"Mmm, this smells so good," Rosa interrupted as she took a small sample of her *madre*'s cooking. "*Grazie*, we'll have it for lunch," she said with a determined smile.

Conversation switched to other things as Maria Giovanna glanced out the window. "I see that the wheat is coming along well. How's Grazia doing?"

"She napping right now, but she is doing well. It's hard to believe that she's already a few months old." Rosa glanced out the window. "It's good the wheat is doing so well; the harvest is only a little while away."

CHAPTER FOUR

Wheat Harvest

"Rosa, what on earth are you doing?" Maria Giovanna exclaimed. "And just what are you going to do with all of this?" she asked as she pointed to the equivalent of several batches of macaroni. Dough was hanging on racks all over the room.

Rosa laughed, and turned from her work on the table. "Must you come by every day, *Madre*?" Dried dough stuck to her flour-coated hands as she crossed the room.

"Yes, actually, I must," Maria Giovanna smiled. "I won't let my only daughter live so close to my own home and not come to check in on her every day. Without Raffaele here, I feel it's my duty to keep an eye on you. Besides," she turned towards the opened window and drew in a deep breath, "summer is in full bloom now, and you have many things to keep you busy. And speaking of keeping busy, would you mind telling me what you are doing with all of this?" Her hand motioned through the air.

"Well, as you can see, I'm baking some macaroni," Rosa smiled, "and since I know you're going to ask, it's for the picnic I host each harvest for the hired hands."

"Ah," mused Giovanna, "I see. Well, anyhow, I just wanted to check on you and Grazia; I'd guess she's sleeping again?"

"Yes," said Rosa, "and I'd better get back to my work and finish as much of this macaroni as I can. She can be pretty demanding when it comes to her mealtimes."

A few days later, and many more batches of macaroni later, Rosa hosted her yearly harvest picnic. "For the hired hands, and for the wheat," she'd say. The wheat was pure gold. Men gathered around at the call of her voice.

"Be sure to eat your full. I have plenty more if this is not enough." Rosa placed platters and bowls on a neatly spread cloth and darted in and out among the men, overseeing their consumption as if she was their mother. To many of them, Rosa could have easily been their daughter, but the hired hands seemed indifferent to the fact as they eagerly crowded around the food, a seemingly endless supply of cheese, tomatoes, sauce, breads and wines waiting to be devoured. The men had tied the wheat stalks into bunches the previous day, and now under the soft touch of the moon, the crowd enjoyed the hearty meal in view of the golden clusters.

"*Tante grazie**," Rosa said to the men. "*Grazie.*"

"No problem," said one man, tipping his hat. "It's my pleasure, ma'am."

"You've done a wonderful job," she was saying to another. "I know Raffaele would be very proud."

"You've done a fine job overlooking us, ma'am. He'd be proud of that, too."

It was late into the night before the voices of the people gathered could no longer be heard. The crowd thinned as another harvest picnic passed. Rosa and Grazia, who had been put to bed hours before, enjoyed a good night's rest. Fall would soon arrive, and winter would find the farm house once again vacated.

Back in America, Raffaele was working away the anniversary of his first year spent in America as a married man, as well as the thirteenth year since he'd left Laurenzana for the first time. Months and months passed by without much of Raffaele's notice, though he managed to send an occasional note to Rosa with some of his hard-earned money enclosed.

It was well over a year later before a change took place in the Marones' monotonous lifestyle. Early in 1899, they were enthused over Raffaele's return to Laurenzana. For Rosa and Raffaele, his visit was a reunion. For little Grazia, it was a complete stranger who stepped foot in her house with little warning.

---

* *Tante grazie (tahn' teh 'grattzja):* thank you very much/so much

CHAPTER FIVE

Family

"Come on, Grazia, take my hand," said Raffaele as he walked slowly beside his daughter.

"No, no, no," hollered Grazia, shaking her head and waving her hands vigorously. "No, no!" Her small feet, enclosed in the handmade footwear that had been crafted by her *Zio** Michele, stomped in childlike defiance.

"Grazia," coaxed Rosa, "c'mon, your *padre** wants to hold your hand."

But Grazia wasn't interested in the least, and Rosa finally had to pick her up. "She'll calm down as time passes," assured Rosa as she turned sympathetically to Raffaele. He nodded as they reached their destination.

Raffaele's presence offered the hint of family that he, Rosa and Grazia had previously lived without. And true to Rosa's word, it didn't take long for Grazia to get over the strangeness of the tall, stern stranger. She even began to call him Papa.

"*Rosa, chi bella Rosa*.*" Raffaele's stern voice softened as he extended a gift towards his wife. Though they had been married three years, this was their first wedding anniversary spent together.

"*Grazie,*" breathed Rosa. "I'm so glad you're home, Raffaele. I guess I didn't really notice how much I missed you until your return."

The passing weeks found Raffaele visiting family and old friends, keeping Rosa and Grazia in his tow all the while. An onlooker would have quickly noticed that the small Marone family was well on their way to prospering in the small hillside community.

Their family unity was beginning to grow, the prosperity of their crops and livestock was on the rise, and their second child was on the way.

But an old villager was quick to remind, "He'll be leaving any day now, that's the way it's always been."

And true to the predictions, Raffaele's ear, trained as it was through years of experience, soon heard America calling out his name. "You be good for your *madre*, Grazia," waved Raffaele, "and help out when the baby is born." Though Grazia responded with an enthusiastic wave, Rosa knew that what was taking place around them was far beyond her daughter's comprehension.

"He'll be back in another few years," sighed Rosa, speaking as much for her own comfort as for Grazia's. But Rosa soon realized that to Grazia, the abrupt departure of the man whom she'd begun to call Papa faded away as quickly as the strangeness of his appearance.

* * *

"*Nonno*, Nonno!*" cried Grazia. She loved it when Maria Giovanna arrived each morning and of course, Maria Giovanna loved Grazia.

"How's my baby today? Are you being good for your *madre*?" The length of Mrs. Pavese's daily visits seemed to grow longer and longer as Grazia grew. "And how is my other baby?" Maria Giovanna smiled as she turned to Rosa.

"Just fine." She patted her growing belly and sighed. "Only a few more months till the baby comes. I feel like I've been running since the day Raffaele left, though."

"That's because you have, Rosa. You're running a farm, keeping the hired hands busy and fed. And as if that's not enough for a young lass like you, you also have a toddler under your feet all day and a new baby almost due. It's a wonder you can keep going. At least when Raffaele was here he was able to carry some of the load. Anyhow..." Conversation continued as daughter, mother and grandmother visited and completed tasks around the house together. Rosa was more appreciative of her mother's daily visits than ever.

The passing months drew the arrival of the new baby closer and closer. On November 16, 1899, Rosa gave birth to Giovanna Marone.

"Another girl; I wonder what Raffaele would think of that," laughed a neighbor.

"He'd be proud," confirmed Rosa. "It's so hard, though, to believe that he went back to America nearly a year ago."

Back in America, the nineteenth century might well have passed into oblivion without much notice from Raffaele. So might his fourth wedding anniversary, or his daughter's third birthday or the coming and going of winter. Typically male, Raffaele lived to work and worked to live. He continued to earn money and send portions of it back to Italy, where Rosa would be soon returning to their summer home in Laurenzana.

Another year of monotonous routine passed as Rosa oversaw the wheat crops planted, celebrated the harvest, managed the status of the livestock, celebrated Giovanna's first birthday, returned to their winter home, and welcomed 1901.

"Papa? He's coming home?" asked Grazia. Little Giovanna played nearby as Rosa busied herself near the large hearth.

"Yes, your *padre*'s coming home. He'll be so surprised at how much you've grown." Rosa turned back to her work as she continued. "You were only two years old when he left; you're such a big girl now, Grazia."

The dong of the village church bells suddenly came through the nearby opened window.

"Ah, time for your prayers. Run along, Grazia, hurry." Grazia was out the door in a flash, her young mind assuming the traditional walk to the church building behind the priest to be more of an early evening activity than a religious requirement.

Rosa shrugged and laughed to herself. "And what will Raffaele say about you," she said, turning to look across the room at Giovanna. "I know, he'll think you're beautiful."

* * *

"Spread those blankets over that way a little more. Like this," Rosa instructed. "Good, now we can put the food out and then we'll be ready to start." She stood back with arms akimbo, inspecting the work. A nod of approval sent the servants on to the next task.

"Looks beautiful, don't you think?" asked Raffaele as he approached his wife. "So rich and gold." His face glowed with satisfaction as he glanced across his fields. The two stood for several minutes drinking in the freshness and peacefulness of the land around them. It was their land, and they could not hide their pride.

"Rosa, Rosa." Rosa started at the call of her name, and turned to see one of the house servants bringing the last culinary item from the wagon.

"*Grazie*," called Rosa, then announced that the meal was ready. The hum of voices continued to ring strong as the hungry individuals hastened toward the food. Another harvest picnic was underway and the summer sun was just beginning to sink out of view. The crowd of hired hands was contented, pleased to have been hired to work for the young Marones.

As always, the oncoming darkness meant that the climax of the evening was only just beginning. Italians were party lovers, big on life, food and drink.

"This hill sure . . . seems steeper . . . than it did earlier today," Rosa observed a few hours later. She and Raffaele, and a number of their servants and hired hands, were climbing the hills back to the village. Bundles of blankets, platters and baskets of the remaining food filled the arms of each. The wagon waited ahead for them.

"Yeah . . . at least you're . . . not carry . . . ing dead weight," huffed Raffaele. In his arms he carried Grazia, who had fallen asleep on one of the blankets. Giovanna had been taken home earlier in the evening and put to bed. "This girl . . ." he continued between gasps of air, "is downright . . . heavy."

Rosa smiled into the darkness and chuckled. "I'm carrying . . . dead weight, too."

"You feel like . . . you're dead, but . . . you're just tired . . ."

"No, really." Rosa stopped to catch her breath. Raffaele stopped too, looking at her by the light of the moon. "We're both . . . carrying dead weight," she said again, another smile creeping onto her face. "Raffaele . . . we're going to have another baby."

* *Rosa, chi bella Rosa (Rosa, chee bell'a Rosa):* Rose, what a beautiful Rose
Nonno (nohn oh): grandmother
Padre (pah' dreh): father
Zio (see oh): uncle

CHAPTER SIX

Extended Visit

"Grazia, please stand still and let me pin this sleeve on you. Listen to your *padre*..." Rosa was kneeling on the floor amid scraps of material, the fire from the nearby hearth offering her light. Its warmth was comforting.

"But Mama, I can't see the pictures from here," Grazia whined.

"Here," said Raffaele, "can you see them now?" He held up the book in his hands as he turned to his daughter. She nodded and he continued the story.

"I like it that you bring us books from America," Grazia interrupted. As interested as she was in the books, her constant interjections were trying Raffaele's patience.

"Grazia, let your *padre* read the story," Rosa whispered.

As Raffaele flipped through pages, he paused at each illustration, his fluency in English a matter of interest. "This is a dog, *d-o-g*," he pointed out, "and this is a book, *b-o-o-k*..."

"Book?" Grazia tried.

"Yes, that's right. And this over here is a hat, *h-a-t*."

"Okay, Grazia," Rosa finally announced, "you can go sit by the fire with your *padre* now. Run along."

Rosa grunted as she pulled her pregnant body off the floor. "I need to work on sewing these new clothes before you completely grow out of the ones you have now. My, you're growing so fast." Rosa sat down and began to work.

* * *

"*Rosa, chi bella Rosa,*" greeted Raffaele as he entered the house a few days later. He took off his coat and settled down with his family. Another winter was at hand, and the Marones were enjoying their winter home again. A servant tending meals and household responsibilities allowed Rosa and the entire family relaxed afternoons.

"Papa, Papa," the girls sang at Raffaele's entrance. They dashed and toddled toward the lanky legs of their father. "Papa, tell us another story. Please, Papa?"

"Go play, go play," insisted Raffaele, waving his hands. "Go play."

"But Mama wants to hear about the thing that flies. Tell us the story about the thing that flies." The girls' unwavering determination gave Raffaele little room to disagree. He glanced at Rosa, whose eyes were sparkling with wonder.

"All right, all right . . ."

The girls plopped onto the floor at their *padre*'s feet with eagerness.

"Back in America, there are a large group of men who call themselves aviators. These men work long and hard days on things they call aeroplanes. The aviators sit in their aeroplanes and take off, and they actually fly up into the sky. I've seen them do it, oh yes, many times. They go very fast and very high, just like real birds."

Rosa's eyebrows rose. She noticed the amusement on her children's faces and decided not to interrupt, yet she wholeheartedly disbelieved her own husband's words.

"Well? That's the end of the story."

"No, no. Tell us more, Papa. About the noises and the sizes and . . ."

"Another time. I'll tell you about it another time; go play. Go on."

Rosa smiled as Grazia and Giovanna reluctantly sidled back to their toys. She was rocking in her chair and rested her sewing on her big belly. "Is it chilly out there, dear?" she asked, turning to Raffaele.

"Mmm, a little." He picked up the paper and began to read to himself. Rosa didn't bother to pursue further conversation but contentedly rocked and sewed. She watched her daughters enjoy their toys as her husband absorbed himself in the local news and events. Rosa was well aware of the fact that their new baby would be arriving soon and a peaceful moment would soon be a scarcity.

The new baby, which arrived a few months later on February 26, 1902, was yet another girl. But Maria Carmella Marone fit perfectly into her new family as Grazia and Giovanna were overjoyed at having a new baby sister.

"Come play, come play," hollered Giovanna.

"No silly, the baby just got born." Grazia's tone of voice was as gentle and motherly as Rosa's would have been. "But when we get home," she declared, "Maria can come and play."

"We'll play outside."

"Yes, and we'll play with the sheep dogs and we can show Maria the big hills and . . ."

Raffaele was annoyed at the girls' constant chatter and waved his hands at them through the air. "Go and play so that your *madre* can rest."

"Tsk, tsk, Raffaele. You're tired of your own children," yawned Rosa with a smile. Raffaele only picked up his newspaper and began to read. "You're just not used to them, that's all."

"No, I guess the streets of New York are more to my liking . . ."

Rosa smiled at his loss of patience, but was too tired to comment. One short year remained before their fourth baby would be conceived. Rosa didn't know it then, but she'd be glad that Raffaele hadn't returned to America yet.

CHAPTER SEVEN

Trouble

"Papa, shouldn't you be going home now?"

"Yeah," echoed Giovanna. Lately, she had fashioned into Grazia's shadow and mimicked her every word and action. Now she sat straight, with her arms rested on the table edge in front of her, gazing at her father. She made an occasional glance towards Grazia, following every motion.

"This is my home," said Raffaele.

Rosa broke into a chuckle. "Grazia," she blurted while her fork stalled in midair, "don't you like your *padre* being here with us?" In her lap Maria squirmed sleepily.

"Well," said Grazia frankly, "he's been here an awfully long time." Her small shoulders slumped in a sigh under her frilly collar. She glanced again at Raffaele.

Raffeale didn't have an answer to Grazia's question, and he changed the subject. "That wheat is doing wonderfully," he observed as he looked out the window. "It will be ready to harvest before you can blink your eye." Grazia began to blink her eyes as fast as she could and then to squint them. Giovanna was watching, and the two made a game out of it. Raffaele didn't notice.

"Yes, it looks like it's already ankle high," said Rosa, trying to eat the rest of her meal while Maria continued to squirm. "Oh, and while I'm thinking of it, yesterday one of the men said that they found that lamb that strayed off a few days ago." She finished the last fork full, slid her dish away from herself and stood to leave the table. "I can tell Maria's tired; I'll go put her down for a nap. Excuse us."

In her absence, Rosa reconsidered her daughter's question. Raffaele's visit *was* dragging on longer than any visit prior, yet she was not in regret. They had been able to spend several wheat harvests, winter holidays and traditions, birthdays and wedding anniversaries, as well as the birth of their new baby, together as a family.

"Perhaps he liked your birth so much," whispered Rosa into Maria's tiny ear, "that he wants to stay for the next one." She smiled as Maria's eyes closed and opened in the rhythm of her rocking. Finally, they closed in sleep, and Rosa rested her baby gently on the bed.

But before the pregnancy was complete, Rosa became dreadfully ill.

"Raffaele, please send the children into the other room to play. I need to rest." Rosa pulled the blankets up to her chin and snuggled deep between the covers. "And can you throw an extra blanket on me?"

Raffaele nodded and turned to the girls. "Now, Grazia, you take Giovanna and Maria into the other room and play," he said seriously. He walked to a nearby chair and took the folded blanket off of it to spread on the bed.

"But Papa, what's wrong with Mama?"

"I don't want to leave Mama."

"Just go like I said, your *madre* will be fine."

Grazia turned away and reluctantly led the trio out of sight.

"Could you stir the fire or something, I'm still cold." Rosa was as deep as she could be in the bed of blankets and Raffaele turned, looking concerned.

"I'm just chilly, Raffaele. Don't worry."

"But you don't look too good. How do you feel?" As Raffaele spoke, Rosa heaved her last meal.

"Look, I'm going for the doctor. Now you lay right there, Rosa, and don't go anywhere. I'll tell the girls to stay in the other room." Raffaele dashed out of sight in a shudder of worry; something was wrong, and his pregnant wife needed help.

"I'm so hot, and everything aches all over," Rosa told the doctor when he arrived. "I'm tired but I can't sleep." She tossed and turned, then heaved again.

The doctor reached for Rosa's head. "You have a bad fever," he said as he pulled a few blankets off. "Raffaele, why don't you put out the fire a bit."

Raffaele did so, and the doctor turned back to Rosa. "I, I think you have smallpox, Mrs. Marone." Deep frown lines framed his eyes as he turned to Raffaele. "She must go into quarantine. Immediately." Rosa and Raffaele glanced at each other, their eyes sharing the same thought. If only they could share one more afternoon walk, one more quiet evening.

"For how long? Our baby is almost due," said Raffaele.

"Yes, I am concerned about that," sighed the doctor. "But this is a pretty bad case, Mr. Marone, and I'd suggest at least forty days."

"Forty days. But . . ."

"Yes, forty days."

"But what about the baby?" Raffaele asked again.

The doctor shook his head. "We can only hope for the best." He picked up his black leather bag and buttoned his coat. "I'll be back again soon, and will keep an eye on your wife and the baby." Rosa and Raffaele shared a last glance. This time, it was worry for the little life that Rosa was carrying that etched their faces.

The doctor was ready to leave, and Raffaele showed him to the door. "Now, please remember that she is extremely contagious at this stage. With the small children, and even you, we just can't take any risks." The doctor raised a finger, "She is not to leave that room, Raffaele, and no one is to enter . . . for forty days."

CHAPTER EIGHT

Forty-day Wait

Behind the closed door, Rosa slept fitfully through one day after another. She went from feeling cold to feeling hot, from feeling like she was going to throw up to feeling hungry. The door between Rosa and her family was tightly shut, keeping in a horrid disease and keeping out her husband and daughters.

"But why can't I see Mama?"

"Mama! Mama!"

"I want Mama, I want Mama, I want Mama!"

"Your *madre*'s sick," said Raffaele, "and we have to let her get better before we can go in and see her."

The doctor's frequent visits only added to the girls' disheartenment. "But the doctor went in, why can't we go in?"

"Can't we go in with the doctor and then come back out?"

"No, no, no. We all have to wait out here until she gets better. That's just the way it is."

"But why can the doctor go in?"

"Because he's helping her get better."

The constant whining and questioning of Grazia, Giovanna and Maria began to take their toll on Raffaele, creating a strong tide which he struggled to stand against. His own desire to be with his wife created another tide.

One evening, the doctor closed the door behind him, and beckoned Raffaele to a secluded area. "Your baby was born early, and . . ." The doctor lowered his head and slowly shook it. "It was stillborn. A . . . son."

Raffaele nodded reluctantly. "How is Rosa faring?"

Once again the doctor shook his head, but he reached out and patted Raffaele's shoulder. "But there's a good chance she'll get better as time passes; we just have to keep hoping."

"How am I going to tell my daughters this?" Raffaele asked in a quiet tone. "They're upset enough already about Rosa being as sick as she is. They haven't even laid eyes on their own *madre* for weeks now." A frown contorted his facial features in a way that made the doctor look away. The happy sounds of the girls playing in the other room reached the men as they stood in silence, and the doctor shook his head.

"I wouldn't tell them right away," he advised. "It would surely crush every last bit of hope that's in their tiny hearts."

Time continued to pass as Raffaele struggled to maintain his composure and keep his family from falling apart. Finally, against all instruction to do so, Raffaele opened the door which the doctor had closed, and passed over the threshold of which he was forbidden. "You could die, Rosa," he explained. "I just want to be with you once more."

Nothing was said of Raffaele's intrusion, or of breaking the quarantine order. But, when the forty days were spent, Rosa didn't feel much better. Grazia, Giovanna and Maria were anxious to see their mother.

"But you said, Papa."

"I said you could see her when she got better. She's not better yet." His own disappointment tainted his words with harshness and the girls retreated to their boring toys.

"It's the baby that she lost," concluded the doctor. "I'll do what I can for her." Five months passed and still Rosa wasn't well. More treatment. More worry. More impatience.

"Is she going to die? What's happening? Can't you do something?" In his own desperation, Raffaele seemed to echo the same questions his daughters were asking.

"I'm at a loss. I just don't know what else to do," admitted the doctor.

To everyone's surprise, Rosa suddenly figured it out. "I'm pregnant," she told the doctor.

The doctor was aghast. "I'm sorry, ma'am, but I'm not going to take you this time."

"What do you mean?" asked Raffaele, hurrying through the house after the doctor. "You can't just leave like that."

"I don't want to be part of this; I'm afraid she might die, Mr. Marone. Goodbye."

Raffaele was left scratching his head, left to scamper around in search of a doctor as the last four months closed in on him. It was already the end of summer, and he suddenly realized that Rosa was getting bigger and bigger every day. He was certain that he did not want to be the one left to deliver their new baby.

Raffaele never did find another doctor, and on October 6, 1904, Michaelina Rosa Marone slipped unassisted into the world. She was named after her uncle Michele. Just like a doll, Michaelina had a curly bunch of delicate hair. Conveniently, just as everything was turning out all right, the doctor returned.

CHAPTER NINE

Remedy

Grazia, Giovanna and Maria were excited about their new little sister, and were very anxious to hold and love her. Raffaele was excited too, but worried about Michaelina. Rosa was still too sickly to produce milk, and yet Michaelina needed it desperately. The oncoming winter found Rosa heating what little milk she could find while Raffaele stood by, his face etched with deep worry and concern.

"Grazia," Rosa would breath in desperation, "run and find milk for Michaelina. Go now, and fast." Any mother within reasonable distance would soon get a knock on her door. On the stoop, Grazia would be waiting to request milk for her baby sister. For endless months, Grazia hurried into the cold of winter with Michaelina in her arms, asking a capable woman to feed her baby sister.

"This can't go on, Rosa," sighed Raffaele late one night. Rosa sat nearby trying to calm her baby's cries. "We can't bring her up on the dependency of another woman's milk."

"But what else can we do?"

Raffaele suggested a nanny goat. "This should give us a consistent supply of milk for Michaelina. We can even bring it back home with us over the summer and won't have to worry about finding another milk source."

Rosa smiled weakly. The months and months of stress and sleepless nights were beginning to take their toll on her already weak body, but Rosa would not give up. The nanny goat produced ample milk, but as Michaelina grew she demanded more and more.

"You're giving her less and less milk every day," said Raffaele. "We can't cut back anymore. She's getting sickly, Rosa. We have to do something different."

Rosa continued rocking Michaelina for several minutes, contemplating her reply. Michaelina's wail of hunger continued to ring in her ears. "I'll give her to the church," she finally stated.

Raffaele started at the sudden suggestion. "Give her to the church?"

"Yes." Raffaele had not come from a religious family, but Rosa had. "And we'll sacrifice everything that we grow this year, too. We have to do it, Raffaele, it's the only way."

"But my fields, my animals. Rosa, I . . ."

"Raffaele, it's for Michaelina," interrupted Rosa. "It's the only way."

The Sovereign Hand that Rosa consulted soon sent its reply. Raffaele watched in surprise as he saw barren chickens lay eggs, his fields and livestock yield abundant, hearty profit. He just as quickly swallowed his pride, though, when Rosa packed it all up.

"For that," laughed Rosa, "Michaelina's going to have a green thumb. I just know it."

"Well, I guess your determination has paid off," said Raffaele one pleasant day in late 1905. He glanced at their girls who were playing in the grass, and Michaelina who sat nearby. "Except now she has to wear that silly little robe," he added with a sigh. The Marones were enjoying a relaxing day in the hills, and had taken a rest in the shade of a tree.

Rosa laughed, and then grew serious. "But she's alive, Raffaele." Her arm reached toward her husband's with poignancy, seemingly overlooking the fact that sacrificing their daughter meant dressing her in peculiar clothing. "We might have lost two children in a row, dear, if we hadn't turned to the church. Besides, it's only a seven-year contract."

Raffaele didn't have a reply, and Rosa followed his gaze into the distance. She knew what he was thinking.

"Raffaele, you can go," she said quietly.

"Go where?"

"Back to America. I know that's what you're thinking about. I can see it in your eyes."

Raffaele nodded. "Yep, I hear her calling." He rested his head back against the large base of the tree and closed his eyes.

* * *

"You're staying here this winter?" Maria Giovanna asked. "But are you sure it's what you want to do?"

"Yes," said Rosa. "It's just too difficult for me to make the trip with all the children."

"Well, it's no true surprise," came a chuckling response. "Just look at you, Rosa, you have three young girls, a toddler, and yet another baby on the way. And on top of that, your husband is thousands of miles away in America."

Truly, Raffaele was thousands of miles away, yet the passing of months spent in hard factory work generated money. Money that, coupled with the assistance that Grazia, Giovanna and Maria lent, though their willingness occasionally left much to be desired, made the farm run most smoothly and efficiently.

On July 6, 1906, Donatine Maria Marone was born. After receiving her fifth daughter, Rosa hit the ground running as she returned to planning meals, mending and sewing clothes, assigning and overseeing responsibilities and keeping livestock and crops in top shape. One of the things not on Rosa's list of things to do, however, was complain. She happily cared for her children and home alike, carefully protecting them both.

"Why don't you walk over to *Nonno*'s and see how she's doing?" Rosa often suggested. "Run along now and play. But do keep your dresses clean."

Donatine was growing quickly, and it was only a matter of time before she was toddling along with Michaelina and ultimately skipping up and down the cobbled streets or through the long grass on the hills. Michaelina and Donatine were always together, like twins, while the older girls had their own playmates and things to do. Many a summer afternoon found them strolling together towards Maria Giovanna's house.

Rosa liked to see her children visiting with their *nonno*. Recently, Giovanna and Maria had begun to spend the nights at an elderly aunt's house to keep her company, and perhaps Michaelina and Donatine felt interested in obtaining similar independence.

"Oh my dears, come in, come in," Maria Giovanna Pavese smiled as she ushered her two small granddaughters into her comfortable home. "You girls sit down, and I'll go find you a treat." Her chubby stature would shuffle gracefully out of sight and return to the table with an array of Italian delights, baked and prepared with her own seasoned hand. Other times, Michaelina and Donatine would watch Maria Giovanna walk towards the door, on the back of which always hung a big bunch of dried figs.

"How would you like some of these today?" she would ask with an excited chuckle. "Huh?"

A smile always passed between the girls as they jumped from their chairs, happy and anxious for the delicious taste of the dried fruit. "Hide them, *Nonno*! Hide them, hide them!" The girls liked to pick up the hems of their dresses so that their petticoat pockets were exposed. "Put them in here, *Nonno*."

Michaelina and Donatine knew that their little cousins, who lived nearby, who also came to get their share of dried figs, complained when they saw Michaelina and Donatine getting some. Back in the safety of their own home, Michaelina and Donatine would eat the dried figs without their cousins ever finding out.

"Michaelina, I have something for you," Maria Giovanna would often say. She would once again disappear and return a few minutes later with a small doll in her hands. "Michele left this for you. Here you are."

The girls would gasp in a dreamlike wonder as they gazed down at the play doll. "She's beautiful. Thank you, *Nonno*. Thank you, thank you."

"Tsk, tsk, tsk. You know that your *Zio* Michele gets those for you, I'm just the go-between in all of this. He's on another trip again until next week, but when he comes back you can thank him yourself. It's kind of him to bring you a gift like this, don't you say?"

"Yes, it's awfully kind of him," said Michaelina.

"Be sure you take care to handle it gently and put it at home with your others," Maria Giovanna instructed.

* * *

"Grazia," called Michaelina. "Can I get a ride on the mule?"

"All right, come on," agreed Grazia. The wheat had recently been harvested and another picnic was underway. "I'll boost you up, but you'll have to hold this dish of macaroni."

"Okay, I can hold it."

"Good," said Grazia. She handed Michaelina the dish and began to lead the mule forward. The mule bumped through the streets of the village as it headed for the hills. Grazia halted the mule as she reached her favorite location; the point where the village streets ended and the green grasses of the hills began. The two sisters could see the golden fields down below. The wheat was all tied in bunches, waiting to be threshed, and the sun was sinking in the background.

"It's such a pretty sight, don't you think so?"

"Yes," said Grazia, "and it's even more beautiful when the moon shines on it." She started up the mule again, but the combination of a steep hill, a top-heavy mule and a large dish of macaroni in the grip of two small hands was not good. They started over the hill and Michaelina suddenly rolled off and fell to the ground, leaving the dish of macaroni to fly through the air.

Had anyone known that Rosa's picnics would soon be coming to an end, something would have been done to change things. In a few short years, Raffaele would be returning, and what his visit would prelude was something that no one ever expected.

CHAPTER TEN

The Unexpected

"I've had enough of your going back and forth to America," reasoned a family member. "You have a wife and children that you are obligated to take care of."

"But I take care of my family," protested Raffaele. "I send them money, and they live here with abundant food, a house and servants and . . ."

"It's not the same, Raffaele. Living hundreds of miles across the ocean is completely different than living in the same house."

Raffaele and Rosa were surprised. Neither of them had ever paid much attention to the locals' buffetings about their separation and neither had ever expected any of them to ever go this far.

"You best break the promise to keep her here," said Maria Giovanna. "I'm getting older, Raffaele, and I would rather see my daughter fully content for at least a few years before I die."

"So, take her to America with me?" Raffaele asked.

Donato gave a slow and reluctant nod.

"Okay, I'll take her back to America with me and we'll stay for say, six years. After the six years, we'll come back here and discuss it further."

"All right, then, six years. But that will be all."

There was much to do. During the winter months the Marones worked hard to prepare for their departure. Raffaele's knowledge gained through past experience helped to discern between necessity and non-necessity, what could be replaced in America and what couldn't. As to the traveling details, Raffaele left those to his brother-in-law.

"Now in this envelope," Michele instructed, "you will find all you need for the trip. Tickets for . . ."

"*Zio* Michele, *Zio* Michele, is there a ticket for me in there?" interrupted one of the girls.

"Yes, there's a ticket in here for each of you. Now, as I was saying," continued Michele with a smile, "I've gathered everything together that you'll be needing." He patted the envelope in his hand and eyed Raffaele. "I know that you're already familiar with the route you'll be taking, but I thought a few peripherals might be helpful to Rosa and the girls."

"*Grazie.*" Raffaele extended his hand to take the envelope and set it on the nearby table. The girls immediately darted across the room and crowded around it. Rosa's quick eye caught their intentions before their hands could even reach for the envelope. "Girls, don't touch, please."

"Yes, Mama," came their reluctant replies, though their eager eyes were taking in every inch of the closed envelope as if their determined stares would reveal the contents. Finally, they turned back to the conversation between their parents and uncle.

"I can't recall the exact dates, but you will be sailing out around the end of March," Michele was saying. "And the departure location, name of the ship . . ."

"But how will we know what date we are to leave?" asked Rosa.

"Don't worry, Rosa. I've written everything down for you. It's all there in the envelope. I was just going to mention that I've written down all the information that I think you'll need, but if you have any further questions you know where to find me. But for now I guess I'll let you return to your work." He picked up his hat and turned to go. "I know you have plenty to do before you're ready to take off."

"*Grazie*," Rosa waved as her brother slipped through the door, then turned towards the others.

"Well, we better hurry up and finish this packing. It's only a matter of weeks before the end of March and . . ."

"We have plenty to do," finished Raffaele. A slight smile broke the sternness of his face. The list of things to bring and tasks to complete before departure were endless. Maria Giovanna kept a close eye on her daughter as the preparations were made, and spent every spare minute alongside her beloved child.

"*Madre*! What on earth have you brought me?" said Rosa as she welcomed her *madre* through the door one afternoon. Maria Giovanna's arms were filled to bursting with baskets, bundles and small boxes.

"Just a few things for your journey."

Rosa took what items she could and placed them on the nearby table and backed away in surprise. "That's enough cheeses, sausages and . . ."

"I want my daughter and her family to be well fed on the journey. You be sure to pack this up well in your luggage and take care that everyone eats a fair share. I don't want to receive news that anyone's taken ill."

"Yes, *Madre*. But . . ." Rosa's voice trailed off as Maria Giovanna disappeared out the door as quickly as she'd come.

"Where is everything else going to go?" finished Grazia.

Rosa turned at her daughter's voice and smiled weakly. "Unfortunately, your *nonno* didn't feel inclined to stay around to answer that question. Oh well, I guess we'll just have to make do. Back to those clothes I was packing," said Rosa as she turned back to her work, "I'm just about through with the hems on Michaelina's and Donatine's new dresses. Here, bring them over to me and we can work on them together."

Grazia crossed the room for the basket of sewing and sat down to begin the work. The two chatted as they worked, their hands moving the needles quickly along.

"These really look wonderful," said Grazia after a while. "Michaelina and Donatine will certainly look fine on our trip to America."

"Yes, that was my exact intention," smiled Rosa. "I think your *padre* did a wonderful job in choosing this cocoa-colored material. It will contrast softly with Donatine's dark hair and olive-skinned arms."

Grazia agreed and tied off her thread just as Michaelina and Donatine entered the room.

"Are they all finished?" asked Donatine. Michaelina was trailing behind her, waving her favorite doll through the air and mumbling to it in petty conversation.

"Yes, they are," said Rosa, "all ready for the journey to America."

"I love it, Mama," said Michaelina, letting her doll drop lifelessly onto the table. "I'm going to have a blue sailor dress for the journey." Then she suddenly stopped and gazed upwards. "But Mama, don't I have to wear the robe that the church gave me?"

"No, dear," Rosa smiled, "the seven years are just about up."

"Mama?"

"Yes, Michaelina."

"Why is all this food on the table? That's enough for many, many meals," said Michaelina with wide eyes. "We can't eat all that before we leave, can we?"

"No." Rosa smiled. "Your *nonno* brought it by just a minute ago and wants us to bring it with us to America. There," she pointed, "it's going in that chest. Actually, why don't you and Donatine drag it over here and we can start packing it. We only leave the day after tomorrow . . ."

The quartet worked the rest of the afternoon until the food filled most of the chest.

"Now, all these clothes fit in these little holes. Oh . . ." Rosa stood and rubbed her back, sighing a deep sigh.

"But Mama," said Michaelina in dismay. She had left the room and was now standing beside the chest with her arms heavily loaded. "My dollies, Mama. What about my dollies?"

"Oh, Michaelina." Rosa looked away, a tear escaping her eye lid. *How can I say no to her?* Rosa thought to herself. She returned her gaze to the bundle of arms and legs that were beginning to escape from the small, loving arms that stretched around them. "Michaelina, there isn't room for them," said Rosa quietly. "I'm sorry."

"But Mama . . ." The hint of a whimper could be heard in Michaelina's voice but Rosa shook her head. Michaelina looked from the bundle in her arms to the doll that she'd left on the table. "Couldn't I bring just her?"

Rosa looked towards the table to see Michaelina's favorite doll, a nun dressed in the traditional garment and head adornments. Again, though with even more heartache and hesitation than before, she shook her head. "I'm sorry, Michaelina."

Grazia and Donatine had been watching quietly. Now as Rosa turned back to her work and Michaelina turned to leave the room, Grazia stepped forward.

"Michaelina, I have an idea. I know it will be sad to leave your dolls behind, but what if you left them in good hands?" Michaelina was puzzled, so Grazia continued. "You could leave one doll to each of your favorite little girl friends, huh?"

"Grazia, that's a wonderful idea," said Rosa. "Michaelina?"

Michaelina's eyes went from her favorite doll to the bundle in her arms to the packed chest. "Okay, Grazia. But I'll give my nun doll to my favorite friend!"

* * *

"*Addio*, Madre*," said Rosa. Try as she might, the flow of tears was too strong to hold back. "*Addio, Padre*. Take good care of our farm while we're gone." A slight smile tried to work its way onto her face as she spoke. "And mind you, keep an eye on the sheep."

"I will, my daughter. I will."

Rosa squeezed her arms tightly around family and friends. Finally, she pulled herself away. "I'll miss you all," she waved. "*Addio*." As the covered wagon drove slowly in the opposite direction, Rosa and the girls waved their final farewells to family, friends and neighbors.

"*Nonno, Nonno, Nonno,*" Michaelina wailed. "I don't want to leave *Nonno*."

"Mama, I want to go back home," cried Donatine. "I'm still

sleepy . . ." She yawned, then wearily rested her head against her sister's shoulder. "I don't feel good, Grazia."

"There, lie down on my lap and go to sleep." Grazia stroked Donatine's hair and watched her sister's eyes struggle between watching her family and friends fade into oblivion and returning to the much desired sleep.

It was very early morning, and the murky darkness, mingled with tears, blurred the parting scene and swallowed the figures and faces as if it were all a bad dream. Rosa turned around in her seat and put the town of Laurenzana behind her. She took a deep breath and tightly shut her eyes, determining to burn the chubby silhouette of her mother and the handsome figure of her father into her mind.

"Write to us," someone called.

"Don't ever forget us," called another.

Raffaele kept the wagon moving at a steady pace, leaving behind the village and its life and civilization. The first few hours of their journey passed quietly as they climbed and descended hills, maneuvered around gullies and rocks. The vigorous rocking and jerking put the girls back to sleep quickly and left Rosa and Raffaele sitting together in silence, concentrating heavily on staying in their seat. Dawn came, and the sun rose higher and higher, soon burning off most of the morning chill. Chirping birds, the pounding of the hooves and rattling of the wheels woke the girls late in the day.

"Why are we stopping?"

"Is this America?"

Raffaele chuckled. "No, this is Naples, Italy." His voice rose as they entered the crowded streets which were swarming with people, buggies, carts and other animals. The girls peered in amazement at the large buildings, cobbled streets, and crowds of people. Never in their young lives had they seen so many people or so much bustling in one place.

"Why are we here?" said Michaelina as Raffaele pulled the wagon to the side of the street.

"We're spending the night here. Tomorrow we'll continue our

journey to Genoa." Raffaele turned to Rosa as he prepared to dismount the seat. "I'll go find us a room and then we can unload. Wait here."

While waiting, Rosa turned in her seat. "Grazia, how's Donatine?"

"Oh, I don't think she's much better," said Grazia as she yawned. "But at least she's getting some extra sleep."

Donatine had slid off Grazia's lap and was in a deep sleep atop the bundles that filled most of the wagon floor. Beside the large family chest, Rosa had packed small bundles in kerchiefs and other pieces of material.

"Mama, what's this place?" said Maria.

"This is a hotel. We're going to spend the night here, but first we have to get a room and unload the wagon."

"What are we going to do after that?"

"Well," said Rosa as she turned in her seat, "first we'll get you something to eat, and then your *padre*'s going to take us to a movie."

"A movie? What's that?" asked Giovanna and Grazia at once.

"It's a show," Rosa explained, "like an act." The girls nodded, but it was evident that they were completely confused. "Then we're going to come back to this hotel and go to sleep. We've got a long journey ahead of us."

It was only a matter of hours before the Marones had unloaded the wagon, filled their stomachs with a hearty meal, sat through a show about snakes and returned to their hotel room for a good night's sleep.

* *Addio (ad'dio):* bye, goodbye

CHAPTER ELEVEN

Old Country Behind, New Country Ahead

At the Genoa harbor of northern Italy, the Marones were greeted with more cool temperatures as they boarded and prepared to sail on the North German Lloyd Liner S S *Prinzess Irene*. On the 23rd of March, they left Genoa for Naples, where they made a quick stop before reaching Palermo on the 26th. A few minutes past 6 P.M. on March 27, the *Prinzess Irene* left from Gibraltar, Spain. Its passengers consisted of 66 first cabin, 156 second cabin and 1,485 steerage, of which 56 were children and 4 were infants.

"Now we're on our way," said Raffaele, "and our next stop is New York, America."

Rough seas, high winds, poor visibility. The first few days of the journey left the *Prinzess Irene* with adverse weather conditions, which made navigation difficult.

"Bulkheads closed," ordered the captain, "soundings to be taken every hour." The deep and weathered tone of Frederic von Letten Peterssen bellowed above the roar of the waves. Though the water spray made the expansive deck slippery, the crewmen executed their captain's orders with haste. Strong winds whipped at their sleeves and pant legs and blew salty drops of water onto their faces. The passengers below, enjoying the conveniences of a large saloon and cafeteria, could feel the rock of the liner as wild waves hit the sides of the boat.

"Giovanna, you need to eat, dear." Rosa sat beside the limp figure of her daughter, fingering a dry roll.

"I can't . . . ooohhh, I feel so sick."

"Maria, how about you, huh? C'mon, you haven't eaten hardly anything . . ."

Maria shook her head wearily.

One long day after another. One sickening hour after another. One long journey that never seemed to come to an end, especially for Rosa. Now six months pregnant, she struggled in the cramped and unfriendly environment. With the upper deck so frequently soaked with the rain and over spray from occasional waves, the passenger compartments on the lower deck became dreadful with the smell of seasickness, body odor and closed in air.

"Here, you rest for a while, Rosa," said Raffaele.

"Yes, everyone else is finally sleeping or at least not throwing up anymore," sighed Rosa. A small smile crinkled her dry lips. "And little Donatine here is the only one besides you who hasn't gotten seasick. Oh, consider yourself fortunate, Donatine . . ."

"The food is yucky, though, Mama. I don't like boat food."

Rosa smiled, but was too tired to reply.

On Tuesday, April 4, the weather cleared around 6:50 P.M., allowing Captain Peterssen to take an observation. "Latitude twenty-nine degrees, twenty-four minutes north," he recorded in his log, "and longitude sixty-three degrees west." The following day, however, brought light rains and haze thick enough to hide the horizon. By 8 P.M., the haze was too thick to continue forward with much speed. "Reduce speed to four knots, soundings to be taken every hour."

Their journey finally nearing completion, the passengers drifted off to sleep below deck. Their confidence in their captain was well-founded on his eleven years as seaman, and four years as captain of the *Prinzess Irene*. Through the night, Captain Peterssen and his crew worked to maintain a safe speed under the hindered navigation. At 2 A.M. Thursday morning, Captain Peterssen, Second Officer Hoennecke and Fourth Officer Vessering were on the bridge, while two lookouts were in the bow and crow's nest.

"Reposition to crow's nest," Captain Peterssen instructed one of the lookouts in the bow. "Keep your eyes open for the Fire Island Lightship," he added.

"Aye, sir."

The haze began to lift, and all trained eyes were peeled. *We should be fifteen miles to the south of the lightship,* Captain Peterssen mentally calculated, *by laying the course five degrees to the north and allowing two degrees for drifting, I believe that we should pass seven miles south of the lightship.*

Minutes later, visibility became marginal and Captain Peterssen could see four or five miles ahead. Open sea filled his vision, clouded only by a small strip of haze. "Full speed ahead," he soon bellowed into the crisp morning air. His crew responded swiftly, and the *Prinzess Irene* began to push through the seas at her maximum speed of fourteen knots. For another hour they pushed towards their destination. "Still no land," breathed Captain Peterssen, puzzled. It was now 3:30 A.M. Standing high above his ship, the wind whipped wisps of hair from his hat and tickled his face. Twenty minutes passed.

Suddenly, at 3:55 A.M., there was a large jolt.

"We're aground," Captain Peterssen cried suddenly. "Cut the engines. Full speed astern." His quick thinking and calm demeanor assisted in his attempt to free his liner from the sand bar. "She's not moving," he finally stated in dismay. Turning to a crew member, he ordered that the deadlights* be lowered. The crewmen didn't have to be told twice, nor did they need an explanation. The passengers would be alarmed if they saw land so close and the possibility of water leakage would be greater.

Below deck the initial jerk of the liner had shaken everything on board and some of the passengers had jumped out of bed in haste and were scurrying around in their night clothes.

"Mama, what happened?" cried Grazia. She had been awakened from a deep sleep and ejaculated the first words that had come to mind.

Donatine suddenly sat upright and began to holler at the top of her lungs, her eyes shut tightly in fear. Bodies of other passengers bumped her in the back and arms jostled her small frame.

"Grazia, gather the bundles," Rosa instructed, now wide awake even in the darkness. Her own uncertainty of the situation tainted her normally calm demeanor with detectable worry. "I don't know what's happened, but it doesn't sound good. Hurry girls."

"Mama, where are you?"

"Over here, grab my hand. Stand close to me . . ." Her outstretched arms flailed in the darkness as her children scampered in the direction of her voice. They stumbled around as the liner shook, rocked and jerked.

"It's all right, ma'am," came a woman's comforting tone. For a minute, none of the Marones recognized the voice, but suddenly Rosa remembered the nun who had befriended them on the first day of the journey.

"Ah, *grazie*," sighed Rosa. "I don't know what's happened, but I am sure worried sick."

"Where's Papa? I want Papa, Mama." Donatine's lower lip quivered and she began to wail once more.

"Shush, shush," said Rosa. "Your *padre*'s in the lower deck with the other men where he's been since the beginning of this trip. Shush now, he'll be up soon."

Suddenly, screams of panic ceased for a split second as electric lights obliterated the darkness. The windows shut simultaneously and plummeted the passengers into deeper fear and uncertainty.

"They're locking us in here."

"What's happening?"

"Where's the rest of my family?"

"Quiet, please! All of you please calm down." The boom of a male voice suddenly struck everyone's attention. "My name is Dr. Ernesto Mensi, and this is my friend, Dr. E. Oteri." The men, an Italian Royal commissioner and Italian surgeon, moved deeper into the crowd, their presence comforting and calming. "The *Prinzess Irene* has run aground . . ."

Mensi and Oteri's calm and comforting tones carefully explained the situation at hand. Before long, the passengers were once again closing their eyes in sleep.

"Well, that wasn't too difficult," said Mensi as they exited the steerage.

Oteri nodded as they turned a corner that led to their berth. "Oh, pardon me," he said with a start.

A man in his night clothes was running full speed in the opposite direction and had nearly collided with the men. They stopped and turned to watch him run wildly down the hall. He suddenly slid to a halt at a particular door and began to knock loudly.

"Wake up, the ship is aground." Bang, bang, bang. "Wake up, the ship is aground."

Finally, a sleepy tone droned through the closed door. "Let her stay aground and go away."

* *Deadlight*: A strong shutter that fits over portholes and cabin windows.

CHAPTER TWELVE

Assistance Needed

Rrrrrring! Rrrrrring! It was 6 A.M. Thursday morning, roughly two hours since the *Prinzess Irene* had hit the sand bar. Now, passengers were sleeping peacefully below deck as their captain made efforts to inform land personnel of his predicament. Rrrrrring! Rrrrrring!

Though thick fog had settled in, the siren carried quickly over the water and reached the small oyster-town of Sayville, Long Island, New York with a shriek. Sailors and lifesavers jumped out of their beds. "A ship must be aground," their experience led them to wager. In between quick bites of an early breakfast, the men gathered and donned their gear. From many different directions, a large handful of capable men prepared to lend their assistance. They eagerly set out in their fishing boats across Great South Bay towards Fire Island.

The moan of the liner's siren had also reached Ed Baker, a lifesaver from the Lone Hill Fire Station who was patrolling his portion of the shore. He quickly telephoned the news to his father, Captain Charles W. Baker, at the Point o' Woods Fire Station. "A large two-pipe transatlantic steamship ashore opposite the life saving station. Looks like a German liner." Shortly thereafter, a second message followed. "*Irene* aground off Lone Hill Life Saving Station, Sayville, S.I. Vessel uninjured and passengers asleep."

Handling the small lifeboats across the Bay was difficult for the seamen, the thick haze and rough seas hindering their abilities to steer and maneuver. Soon enough, though, the Sayville men reached the shores of Fire Island. Running their boats to the opposite beach, lifesavers were rushing in from all directions, spurred by the possibility of immediate rescue. The men called to one another above the roar of the waves as they made preparations. The morning light was dim and obscured, a chill breeze nipping at exposed skin.

Among the lifesavers was Captain George E. Goddard, and his small crew, from the Lone Hill Life Saving Station. They dove into their boats before any of the other men, and were the first to set off toward the *Prinzess Irene*. Coming to Fire Island as a stranded seaman himself, Captain Goddard had been a dedicated lifesaver since 1871. His quick reply to Captain Peterssen's plea for help, and his presence among the first lifesavers to gather on the shore, proved his concern.

Now, while Captain Peterssen busied himself aboard his liner sending a notification wireless telegram back to shore, Captain Goddard and crew were making their way through the fog. "Heave!" cried Captain Goddard. "Hard on the right. Heave! Heave!" Water from the waves rolled off the men's oil skinned suits unnoticed. Their minds were concentrating on their seemingly counterproductive efforts. Pull, pull, pull. The sting of the freezing salt water, the rush of strong waves and the chill in the air made the task difficult and, had they not been highly experienced seamen, they are likely to have capsized.

7:45 A.M. Captain Peterssen sent a wireless telegram to his company's pier at Hoboken, simply stating that the *Prinzess Irene* was aground. A response was quick in coming, both at the pier and the company's Broadway office. Captain Kunwich, pier superintendent of the North German Lloyd Line, jumped aboard the *John Nichols* tug, which was already on its way to the stranded liner, and assured his fellow men at the pier that he'd see to the safety of the passengers. "I'll be back when she's afloat," he said with a wave of his hat.

9 A.M. Perhaps it was the thick fog, or the concentration with which Captain Peterssen was engaged in his communication with land that kept his attention from the lifesavers. While Captain Peterssen was busy requesting wrecking boats and tugs, Captain Goddard was just coming into view of the stranded liner.

A loud hum of excitement and indecipherable blur of dialects reached the ears of the lifesavers. High above them, the passengers of the *Prinzess Irene* had anxiously been waiting for assistance to be sent from shore, and now lined the rails to watch the lifesavers. The *Prinzess Irene's* crewmen were waiting with the davit drops* ready. After repetitive attempts to board the liner amid the rough seas, Captain Goddard successfully got his life boat connected to the davit drops.

"Heave, heave, heave, heave." The *Prinzess Irene's* crewmen slowly hoisted up the lifeboat. In responding welcome to the arrival of the lifesavers, the passengers offered a loud and boisterous cheer.

"Thank you," greeted the men as they stepped out of their boat and onto the *Prinzess Irene*. Water rushing off of them made puddles at their feet. Turning to Captain Peterssen, the lifesavers introduced themselves; in addition to Captain Goddard, there was Ed Baker, Frank Robinson, Bill Flynn, Bill Leach, Jem Oakley, Jr. and Jim Reynolds. Bill St. Clair had stayed on shore to handle communications between shore and the rest of his crew once they boarded the *Prinzess Irene*.

The captains began to analyze the situation at once, and agreed that there was no immediate danger. "No need to risk transferring the passengers right now; just look at those waves."

Destined to wait, and compelled to do nothing more, the lifesavers began to mingle with the crowd of passengers, offering encouragement and support when they could. Until the fog lifted enough to send a wigwag* signal back to shore, Captain Goddard spent his time pacing the deck and fidgeting restlessly. Captain Peterssen on the other hand, kept his mind focused on his wireless telegrams with those ashore. An emergency rescue was not needed for his passengers, but his liner was waiting to be freed.

Thirty minutes passed and still no tugs. Captain Peterssen sent a wireless telegram back to shore, verifying that they had truly been sent his way. Shore responded with an affirmative. In another message soon after, Captain Peterssen informed those ashore that the fog was beginning to lift. The clearing weather heightened his hopes and he added, "I expect to get off the sand about noon." He sent another message at 10 A.M. to say, "*Irene* resting easily. Weather and sea favorable. Expect tugs hourly. Passengers well."

Via telephone, an officer at the Lone Hill Life Saving Station confirmed to another, "The *Prinzess Irene* is about 250 yards off shore, and the weather conditions are good."

"Still waiting for tugs," Captain Peterssen restated more than once.

* * *

"We just might need that breeches buoy*," observed Ed Baker, and with Captain Goddard's approval, he mounted the bridge. High above the deck, and in good view of Fire Island, Ed Baker sent a wigwag signal requesting that the buoy be prepared. Captain Charles W. Baker, in charge during Captain Goddard's absence, replied with an affirmative.

The clearing fog created a view that the *Prinzess Irene*'s passengers had previously only heard about. Before them now stretched the yellow strand of land that formed Fire Island. From their position behind the liner's rails, the passengers could see scores of individuals crowding the beach, townspeople from Sayville and lifesavers from the various life saving stations.

2 P.M. The tugs began to arrive. The derelict destroyer, *Seneca*, reached the *Prinzess Irene* first. "The seas are too rough to go any closer," confirmed the *Seneca*'s crew as they peered over the rails. Down below the rough seas were crashing in violent waves against the vessel. "We'll have to use the small boats."

The men lowered a boat down into the water and watched as the selected lifesavers rowed with all their might. As they looked over the rails of the *Prinzess Irene*, Captain Goddard and his men recalled their own pains to row against the waves. The onlookers from shore peeled their eager eyes. They could see the powerful currents send the small boats speeding up one side of the huge waves and crashing down the other. After a few minutes, the men from the *Seneca* called their crew in the lifeboat back. Obediently, though quite disappointedly, the men paddled back to their tug.

It was another hour before the next tug arrived and a nerve-racking wait continued for Captain Peterssen and his passengers. Back on shore, the telephones were ringing wildly as people called to inquire about the situation. Officials did their best to keep the callers calm and free from worry. Rumor had it that the *Prinzess Irene,* and the passengers aboard her, was in no danger, and that lifesavers and other seamen were working towards freeing her from the sand.

3:30 P.M. Captain Peterssen sent another wireless telegram to shore: "Tugs *Merritt* and *Timmons,* the *Relief,* cutters *Seneca* and *Mohawk* alongside now, tug *Rescue* expected noon today." The *I.J. Merritt* had been sent from New London, Connecticut; the *Mohawk* and *Seneca* from the United States Revenue Cutter Service off Staten Island, and the *Relief* from the Merritt-Chapman Wrecking Company in Tompkinsville.

Upon its arrival, the *Relief* tried to get a line aboard the *Prinzess Irene.* As the *Seneca* had done shortly prior, a handful of men boarded a small boat that was lowered into the vicious waters. They succeeded in getting aboard, and used the line that now stretched between the *Prinzess Irene* and the *Relief* to get underway. Meanwhile, the crew aboard the *Prinzess Irene* had put the stern anchor overboard, which Captain Peterssen planned to use as a warping line*.

"Aye, that there sea and wind have slowed," observed one weathered seaman to another. The shrinking waves were easily observed by all and the momentary lack of chilling breeze appreciated. "Right perfect for haulin' her out."

All eyes were focused on the *Prinzess Irene* as the *Relief* fired up her engines and began to move away from the liner. The line between the vessels began to straighten as it grew tighter and tighter.

C'mon my girl, pull out of the sand. C'mon!

"Full speed ahead," ordered Captain Peterssen. "Full speed and we can pull her out." The liner began to shudder at the strain of her engines.

C'mon, c'mon . . .

---

* *Wigwagging:* With the use of one flag (a red flag with a white center if the user is standing against a light background, a white flag with a red center if the user is standing against a dark background) three motions are used to indicate the dashes and dots of the Morse Code and the end of a sentence or paragraph.

Warping line: A small cable used to move sea vessels.

Davit drops: A crane-like device aboard ships used to lower, raise and support anchors, smaller vessels, etc.

Breeches buoy: A device used to rescue passengers from stranded vessels. Strung between the stranded vessel and land, or between the stranded vessel and another ship, a strong line suspends a chair. The name of the buoy may derive from the canvas breeches into which the rescued individual placed his legs while pulleys drug the chair toward safety. As was the case with the *Prinzess Irene*, a specialized gun is often used to shoot the buoy line to the stranded vessel.

CHAPTER THIRTEEN

Stranded

Men on the *Relief* were as anxious as everyone else. Their eyes glued to the line running between the vessels, someone suggested a winch. "Maybe if we can take in some of that slack, we'll have a better chance of moving her." Yet the passing of time and effort proved futile. After an hour's work and approaching darkness, the efforts were abandoned.

"We'll try again, though," the men solaced.

7 P.M. Captain Peterssen wearily telegraphed a final message before night fell completely: "Ship resting easy, clear, little wind, a good swell on. Passengers comfortable; no danger." Though the *Prinzess Irene* was listing slightly to port, she was deeply embedded in the sand, thus it was not the safety of his ship that worried Captain Peterssen, rather the futile effort to free her from the sand.

Captain Goddard sent a wigwag signal ashore, saying that he and his crew would spend the night aboard the *Prinzess Irene*. As night continued to fall, twenty mile an hour winds began to blow against the liner, causing rough waves to heave sand against her forefoot and stem, also burying her keel yet leaving her starboard propeller only half submerged. One by one the passengers on the *Prinzess Irene* would soon be put to sleep by the gentle sway and rock of the liner. The lights outlining the vessel could be seen from shore bobbing up and down in the darkness.

The seclusion of his cabin provided Captain Peterssen with little more than respite from the weather. Gazing out his window, he could see Fire Island, and six miles beyond that, the lights of Sayville. Recently lit bon fires were flickering on the beach, each surrounded by small groups of spectators. Men, women and children had flocked to Fire Island at the news of a stranded boat and they were determined to remain in view of the liner until the problem was completely solved. Lifesavers and other sea personnel, with their lifeboats ready, roamed the beach with the spectators, whiling away the time by small talk of past shipwrecks andstranded vessels.

But the people crowding around the bon fires were not on Captain Peterssen's mind. Nor were the lifesavers or their lifeboats. *I have sailed over this identical course three different times*, his thoughts played. *This time I took the same sounding and the same reckoning as I did then.* He recalled the open sea that he'd observed during the early morning hours. *Could it be that Long Island had been standing behind the thin cloud of haze?* Captain Peterssen shook his head as he turned from the window, trying to push the reality from his mind.

As if the change of location would help, Captain Peterssen left his cabin to saunter the decks of his ship. The chilly air stung as it whipped at his face and hands. He did not even notice the passengers as he wove in and out among them. His thoughts were deep and focused. *I simply cannot understand how this has happened.*

On another portion of the deck sauntered the Marones, where they were getting some fresh air before they went below deck for bed. The shore line of Fire Island was clearly visible to them in the darkness, peppered as it was with bon fires and crowds of people. Above stretched a clear sky, filled with millions of specks of light.

"Papa, look at all the stars!" Donatine gazed. "Oh they're so bright!" The other girls joined her at the rail, though Raffaele smiled to himself in the dark, shaking his head. He hated to spoil their glee, but knew as well that his reply would beckon greater excitement.

"Those aren't stars, my dears," he said. "They're lights."

"Lights?"

"Yes, from America."

"From America? Oh, hurrah!"

Rosa stood nearby, her quiet smile sharing their joy.

Friday, April 7, 1911 Amid a slight haze and a brisk wind from the southwest, the lifesavers and spectators continued their wait on Fire Island. Their fires were dimming in the early morning light, and breakfast with some coffee chased away the cold. A walk to the waterfront to take another look at the *Prinzess Irene* limbered their tired bodies.

8 A.M. Captain Goddard and his crew left the *Prinzess Irene* as the sun, no longer obscured by the fog, began to burn away the haze. The white capped waves that danced about, adding a bit of cheer to the possibly discouraging situation, were a wink compared to the waves the lifesavers had battled against almost twenty-four hours earlier. Upon reaching Fire Island, the men hauled their boat out of the water. "Any news? How are things back on the liner? Is everything okay?"

Captain Goddard chuckled at the anxious inquisitions that came from the onlookers, but tuned out as he and his crew busied themselves deeper inland. In case usage of the breeches buoy became necessary, Captain Goddard had strung a line to the *Prinzess Irene* and taken the loose end into his lifeboat. Now on shore, he and his men left it ready and waiting.

Grabbing a bite to eat, Captain Goddard and his men settled into conversation with their fellow seamen. "Captain Peterssen and his crew are going to transfer their passengers today. The ship, the *Prinz Friedrich Wilhelm*, left its port at seven this morning and sent a telegram to Peterssen just a little while ago. They should be arriving soon," said Captain Goddard with a glance over his shoulder. His back still to the sea, he turned back to continue his conversation.

"That's great," said the lifesavers who had gathered. "How are the passengers taking this whole situation by the way?"

"Oh, the passengers? Ha, they're perfectly fine!" Captain Goddard chuckled with his crewmen as they recalled the scene back aboard the *Prinzess Irene*. "Initially they were a little nervous, which is to be expected."

"Well, sure," agreed the men.

"Last night I saw many of them playing bridge in the saloon, or playing and singing at the piano."

"And there were concerts, too, given by the band. That livened things up a bit."

"And," said a crewman, lifting his finger, "Dr. Somebody . . ."

"Dr. Mensi?" asked Captain Goddard.

"Yes, Dr. Mensi. Anyhow, he and another man, the two are friends you see, have been working with the passengers and explaining the whole situation." The seaman paused to take a bite of his breakfast. "Anyhow, he said that he hoped Americans would realize how well the inexperienced immigrants have behaved regarding all of this. He really thinks they're taking it well."

"Yeah," laughed another seaman. "Considering the fact that they have been in waiting for nearly ten hours."

A lifesaver nearby was asking about the liner's captain.

"He looks like an old man, to be honest with you," said Captain Goddard. He took a gulp of coffee. "The grounding is certainly weighing heavily on his mind, though, and he just keeps shaking his head about the whole thing."

"So has a definite cause been determined?" asked a fellow seaman.

"I think it might be easier for Peterssen if there was," sighed one of Captain Goddard's crewmen. "The fact that he has sailed this course a number of times before simply has him baffled . . ." Onlookers had begun to gather around when Captain Goddard arrived, and the words passed between him and the other seamen were gathered and passed quickly through the throng.

"I saw his log, though," added Captain Goddard. "He had recorded in there that just prior to hitting the bar, he had marked eighteen fathoms*, going at a speed of fourteen knots. And I don't doubt his speed one bit because I know there isn't a depth of eighteen fathoms within many yards of that bar."

When the breakfast bugle sounded back on *Prinzess Irene*, news of the transfer circulated quickly as the passengers gathered into the cafeteria.

"A boat called the *Prinz Friedrich Wilhelm* is on its way this very minute," said one passenger to another. "And the best part is that everyone is going to be taken to New York on it."

If things went well, the transfer would be made in little time. The *Prinz Friedrich Wilhelm* was bringing representatives of the Port Health Office to examine the passengers, and customs and immigration men to expedite the passengers' landing and baggage examination.

"But the seas have to calm a bit," one passenger noted, "before even one passenger can leave this ship. I know the officials won't let anything begin until those waves die down."

Back on shore, Captain Goddard made preparations for the transfer. "The *Prinz Friedrich Wilhelm* should be arriving soon."

"Let's get all three of the Lone Hill Station's lifeboats down to the beach. That way they'll be ready to launch as soon as we're needed."

* *Fathom*: A unit of length equal to six feet.

CHAPTER FOURTEEN

Farewell, *Prinzess Irene*

12:00 P.M. While Captain Goddard was getting his lifeboats ready, Captain Peterssen was observing the *Prinz Friedrich Wilhelm*'s appearance at the horizon. The *Prinzess Irene*'s crew immediately raised their signal flag, sending "F.I." back to shore. Captain Goddard interpreted the coded message to read, "Send a boat suitable for landing passengers." He glanced at his men, and they responded quickly.

The *Seneca* and *Mohawk* also interpreted the message from Captain Peterssen. They did not grasp his intentions, however, and began to offer their own services. Before they actually let any of their lifeboats into the water, though, Captain Peterssen quickly sent a second message to reiterate his desires. The men decoded the message "S.O.R." to read, "Send from shore."

In turn, Captain Goddard and his men made final preparations to depart for the *Prinzess Irene*. Dressed once again in their sou' westers*, oilskins and high boots that nearly reached their hips, Captain Goddard and his crew approached the water. Six men to a boat side, the men waited until the waves died enough to run their boats into the water. As they waited, a gigantic wave crashed ashore, sweeping each of them off their feet and filling their boats with water.

A few chuckles from onlookers accompanied the men as they dumped the water out of their boats and returned to wait. Captain Goddard's patience paid off, and after six tries he and his men were finally on their way. In Captain Goddard's boat, he stood in the stern sheets* manning the oar and headed his men straight for the *Prinzess Irene*.

As Captain Goddard reached the *Prinzess Irene,* the *Prinz Friedrich Wilhelm* was quickly approaching. Captain Goddard and his men pulled along side the stranded vessel and settled under her lee where the water was calmer. When the *Prinz Friedrich Wilhelm* had reached eight fathoms, Captain Prehn ordered his men to set anchor. His ship was about a mile from the *Prinzess Irene* and about three miles off shore. The *Prinzess Irene's* passengers gave a loud cheer at the sight of the *Wilhelm* and those on shore could easily hear the excited cries across the water. A yawl* from the *Seneca* pulled up beside the *Wilhelm,* posing as a patrol and guard against accident. The afternoon would later reveal that she would not be needed in that regard, so the *Seneca* assisted in other ways.

When the *Prinz Friedrich Wilhelm* had dropped its anchor, Captain Peterssen sent a wireless telegram to his liner's sister ship. "I'm ready to transfer my passengers to your ship." He added, however, that he had some doubts as to the advisability of such an attempt. "The seas are awfully strong."

"Wowee," whistled a crewman from the *Prinzess Irene.* "Will ya look at all those onlookers?" He nudged the shoulder of a fellow seaman, and they both turned towards the beach.

"Why it looks like all of Sayville has come to watch," the man laughed.

"And I'll bet ya they are mighty pleased over all this sudden fame that's landed on their shoulders."

"Well sure," agreed a third man, "they're just a little 'ol oyster town on normal occasions."

Coming to Fire Island during the night and early morning hours, the onlookers had taken oyster boats, rowboats, motor boats and any other craft that was available. To their dismay, they had soon reached shoal waters* that created an undesirable distance between them and the *Prinzess Irene.* An old fisherman however, quickly solved the dilemma, offering his shoulders to transfer each individual across the extra 100 feet. No one was left without a good view.

Back on shore, Captain Charles W. Baker, and his crew from the Point o' Woods Life Saving Station, loaded their boat onto a beach cart. With the help of fifty other men, they drug the cart across Fire Island, where they entered and launched their lifeboat. They were headed straight for the *Prinzess Irene*.

Meanwhile, the lifesavers back at sea were discussing the best and safest means of transfer. Normally, they would have transferred the passengers from the deck of the *Prinzess Irene* directly to the deck of the tugs, but with the heavy seas, the scenario was improvised.

"What do you say we go boat to boat, instead of liner to liner?" suggested one lifesaver.

"Aye, that would be safer, and easier too," agreed another. "That ladder is a pain to rig . . ."

"From the *Irene* to the lifeboats, from the lifeboats to the tugs, from the tugs to the *Prinz Friedrich Wilhelm*," sang a lighthearted lifesaver. At half past noon Captain Goddard left the *Prinzess Irene* to prepare his lifeboat to receive passengers. A few of his men joined him, and crewmen from the *Prinzess Irene* lowered an accommodation ladder, which hung down to the lifeboat at a forty-five-degree angle. The waves rocked the lifeboat roughly up and down and side to side, as if to create as disagreeable a welcome as possible for the passengers.

The entire load of passengers squeezed onto the *Prinzess Irene*'s deck like sardines in a can. One thousand, seven hundred twenty people waiting to be transferred. One thousand, seven hundred twenty people anxious to watch the event unfold.

*   *Stern sheets*: The designated area in the back of an open vessel for the person in command or for passengers.
    Shoal waters: Shallow water
    Yawl: A two-masted sailing vessel.
    Sou' wester: A waterproof hat with a broad flap at the back, usually made out of heavy oiled or painted cloth.

CHAPTER FIFTEEN

Hello, *Prinz Friedrich Wilhelm*

The women and children from the steerage were called first, and as the first passenger, an Italian woman named Priscilla Demello, left the *Prinzess Irene* a loud cheer could be heard from the beach. At the bottom of the ladder, one of the brawny lifesavers caught Demello in his arms and the other lifesavers led her to the other end of the boat. There she sat safely out of their way. Next came three-month-old Mollie Leonie and seven-year old Antonio Deniello. More children continued to come, and Michaelina and Donatine were the first of the Marones to leave the *Prinzess Irene*.

"No Mama! Don't let them take me, Mama!" But the lifesavers ignored their cries as they transferred the immigrant children from the *Prinzess Irene*. The youngsters soon found themselves being placed safely in a lifeboat by the strong and steady lifesavers. The seamen were big and brawny, yet gentle at the same time.

"There, see? It's not so bad after all." Once again, it was the voice of the friendly nun that came as a comfort to the small girls. "First they'll take all of the children to that new boat over there," the nun pointed, "and then they'll come back and get all the adults."

"But you're not a girl," said Donatine over the rush of the waves. Her small hands were glued to the nearest stationary portion of the boat. Out of the corner of her eye she was watching the experienced seamen seated close by her maneuver their boat so well.

The nun chuckled. "You're right, I'm not a child. But for safety's sake, they have decided to fill each boat with children and one adult. Are you sorry I came along in your boat?"

Michaelina and Donatine answered so emphatically that the nun involuntarily fell into another fit of laughter. "Yes, riding in this lifeboat is definitely an interesting experience," offered the nun. Under her breath, and only loud enough for the two children directly at her sides, the nun added, "I would wager that riding in a sea like this is scary even for these here seaman, never mind the rest of us."

From the lifeboat, the girls boarded one of the tugs and were emptied onto the big deck of the *Prinz Friedrich Wilhelm*. There they huddled together and waited for their parents and siblings to arrive.

"My dress is wet," said Donatine with a pout in her voice. "And yours is all wrinkled."

"I don't care," sighed Michaelina. "Besides, I've been wearing this dress since last night; if the boat had just landed like it was supposed to then we would be in America now, and our new dresses that Mama made would look very pretty and nice."

The girls' collars and skirts whipped in the wind as they stood by the rail. Michaelina rested her head on the metal bar and for a split second wished she were back home in bed. Around them buzzed hundreds of other passengers who were speaking strange words. Other passengers were calling to each other and seamen were hollering orders. In addition, reporters from *The New York Times* newspaper darted here and there with note pads, stopping to question different passengers.

Back on the *Prinzess Irene*, the passengers walked past Captain Peterssen before departing, waving farewell and shaking hands with him.

"Cap'n, you're doing a wonderful job!"

"I sure admire you, sir."

"Keep up the good work, Captain."

Captain Peterssen was surprised, though he appreciated the praise.

"Thank you, thank you all."

"I sure hope you get your ship free soon."

"My family and I wish you the best of luck, Captain."

The expressions were endless, and much more than Captain Peterssen had ever expected.

Eleven lifesavers were present to man the ladder and assist the passengers as more continued to descend the ladder. When the lifeboat was filled, Captain Goddard signaled his full load and pulled away. The *John J. Timmons* had pulled into a parallel position behind the *Prinzess Irene,* where the seas were calmer, and the lifesavers steered their boats in a long line from liner to liner. The process now reversed, another accommodation ladder was let down to the lifeboat as the lifesavers assisted one passenger after another up to the tug's deck. The *John Nichols* was also standing by, waiting to fill her decks with passengers.

On a few occasions, the lifesavers were compelled to force a few of the passengers to leave the lifeboats or offer in-depth assistance in ascending the ladders. The children were not the only ones to put up a fight as the transfer continued.

"Don't take me, don't take me off without my luggage!" cried men and women alike. The men were especially determined, seemingly more concerned about their larger chests of belongings than they were about their own lives. Several lifesavers and seamen worked together in persuasion.

"Come on now, they'll take good care of your things."

"I don't care; I won't leave without my luggage."

"Look, they're going to get all of you onto the *Prinz Friedrich Wilhelm* and then they'll take off every piece of luggage, too."

"The sooner you cooperate, the sooner we'll be able to get you and your luggage to New York."

The women worried over being left behind, and another group of lifesavers were busy keeping them in line. With the help of a bilingual passenger, a Mrs. G. B. Stone, the concerned women were quieted.

"I don't want to be left behind."

"They're going to take the cabin passengers and leave us here."

"No they wouldn't do a thing like that. Your turn is next, just be patient."

As this process continued, Captain Peterssen had a one o'clock appointment to meet. In the privacy of his cabin, he was being interviewed by a reporter from the *New York Times*. In the lengthy interview, Captain Peterssen spoke openly of the ten-day journey that had led to the grounding. Pen scribbling furiously, the reporter captured every detail as Captain Peterssen went on to describe the fog that hindered his observations and made navigations difficult.

Captain Baker and his men soon arrived at the scene. Captain Goddard's boat had been filled with another load of ten women and a baby while Captain Rourke, from the Blue Point Life Saving Station, moved in line to wait with his lifeboat. When his boat had filled with more of the *Prinzess Irene*'s passengers, he moved forward to allow Captain Baker's boat to be filled. Before too long, with the additional help from the *Mohawk, Seneca, Relief* and *I.J. Merritt*, there were ten lifeboats assisting in the transfer.

"No, I won't get off this boat until the steerage have all departed first," bellowed a stubborn first-class passenger. A few of the lifesavers exchanged glances and then tried again.

"Just come on, we aren't doing this in any particular order."

"I'm not leaving before they do."

Other passengers from first and second class began to join them, and soon the lifesavers had no choice but to comply. Strangely enough, the first and second class passengers' attitudes were the same as steerage when it became their turn to descending the ladders.

"And you'd think they would at least be either more brave or more scared than the steerage," said one lifesaver to another. Under his breath he added, "They have all jumped over the rails with the same amount of courage." They shook their heads in confusion, but continued their work without skipping a beat.

"Well, they probably don't even know exactly what has happened here," laughed one seaman.

"Yeah, they probably just think this is the way they get to land. The language barrier seems to have left most of them in the dark."

"Ha, you're right. But they do seem to be hugging their babies closer to themselves, more so than the average immigrant," one observed. "Maybe they do know that something's up."

As the afternoon wore on, it was determined that the risk the rough seas posed on the small lifeboats was too great. So, the *John J. Timmons* and *John Nichols* pulled alongside the *Prinzess Irene* and filled their decks in turn. The accommodation ladder was rigged up, and the passengers were called to descend.

"Ha," laughed one lifesaver, "and ya wonder if those first and second passengers were just determined to let the steerage leave first . . ."

"Or were they lookin' to avoid the lifeboats?" interrupted another. The men chuckled together as they began to assist the passengers directly from the decks of the *Prinzess Irene* to the waiting tugs. The tugs proved to work well, the captains executing superb maneuvers amid the rough seas, and the transfer continued smoothly.

Only one scream was heard by those ashore, and a reporter from the *New York Times* who was at the scene would later inform the public by way of his newspaper: A woman from Naples . . . shrieked so loud that every one thought her baby had fallen overboard. Instead, it was only a paper box containing a faded straw hat tied with pink ribbons that had evidently seen many summers. It was recovered and she smiled again.

"It's sure taking a long time," sighed a woman to her friend. Though the many onlookers on Fire Island were eager to watch every minute of the event, the hours were crawling by.

"Aye, it seems like the tugs sit beside the *Prinzess Irene* for hours before they pull away and head for her sister ship."

An experienced seaman suddenly appeared. "Pardon me, miss," he said sheepishly. "I couldn't help, uh, hearin' your conversation. You know, uh, about the transfer . . ." His drawl and averting eyes were a definite distraction, but the women split their attention and waited to hear him out.

"Now ya see here. Those tugs there, the uh . . . *Timmons* and um . . . *Nichols*. Well anyhow, they uh, are real big, ya see. They have large decks, and uh . . . can carry a lot of people, ya know?"

The women nodded as he continued. "And so, uh . . . they can really get a lot of, uh, work done . . ."

The *New York Times* would later confirm the tugs' usefulness. The *John Nichols* and *John J. Timmons* carried their loads, varying in size ranging from 203 passengers to 414, through the waves towards the *Prinz Friedrich Wilhelm,* where the quarantine doctor waited. "Eyes are looking good. Let me see those teeth, open wide." The doctor executed his routine examinations over and over again as the 1,720 passengers reached the *Prinz Friedrich Wilhelm* one by one.

5:00 P.M. The last passenger was put aboard the *Prinz Friedrich Wilhelm* as evening made its appearance. Captain Goddard had made twelve trips from the bow to stern of the *Prinzess Irene,* ferrying 216 passengers, Captain Baker had made seven trips, ferrying 116 passengers and Captain Rourke had ferried 250 passengers. On the contrary, the tugs transferred the remaining passengers to the *Prinz Friedrich Wilhelm* in a total of only six trips. The transfer of the entire 1,720 passengers from the *Prinzess Irene* had taken five hours, with ten minutes intervening, and the time went down in the books as the shortest on record. Back on the Fire Island, circles of seamen discussed the speed and details of the transfer for hours on end.

"Everyone remembers the 'ol *Republic,*" said a seaman. His pipe hung from the corner of his mouth, giving him the looks of an old sea captain.

"Oh yes, she sank off No Man's Land, huh?"

"That she did," replied the old man. He coughed a deep-chest cough before he continued. "And she only had eight hundred passengers, but it took about eight hours to empty 'em all out and bring 'em to safety."

The younger man whistled. "How long ago was that, anyhow?"

"Oh, a might two years I'd reckon . . ."

Dinner on the *Prinz Friedrich Wilhelm* was devoured by the

hungry passengers who were eager, no doubt, to be off the stranded liner and on their way to New York. Loud conversation filled the ears of each individual as persons around them recalled the whole incident. At the same time, engaging in conversation was difficult, as frequent cheers went up as the passengers expressed their opinions and feelings of their captain's skill and expertise.

Back at the *Prinzess Irene*, the *John J. Timmons* was filling its decks with luggage.

"Those immigrants will sure love us for this load," laughed one of the men in the assembly line. He took the first piece of luggage, a Parisian hatbox, and passed it to the next man. Tightly packaged crates, boxes, bundles, valises and chests followed, and moved from liner to tug as the evening progressed.

"A-up, and they'll no doubt sleep peacefully tonight, knowing that their belongings are on the same sea vessel as they are."

The tug was soon filled, and it pulled away. "It's good we were able to get most of the luggage over in one trip; I'm about ready to pack it in."

"Mmm, a hearty meal and a warm bed sound good to me."

With dinner now finished, the passengers lined the rails of the *Prinz Friedrich Wilhelm* as their individual belongings came into view aboard the tug. Out of the dimness, the approaching tug chugged towards the *Prinz Friedrich Wilhelm*.

Complete darkness had fallen by the time the *Timmons* had finished unloading the baggage from the *Prinzess Irene*. Out of determination to not lose sight of their precious belongings, the passengers stood crowding the rails of the *Prinz Friedrich Wilhelm* until the *Timmons* was finally on its way.

9:07 P.M. Now filled with passengers and baggage, the *Prinz Friedrich Wilhelm* sailed off into the night. Captain Prehn headed for Robbin's Reef, where his liner would drop anchor and spend the night. Behind them in the darkness, the passengers watched as Captain Peterssen and his 380 officers and crewmen grew invisible. The superstructure of the *Prinzess Irene* was soon swallowed in darkness.

CHAPTER SIXTEEN

Arrival, Rescue . . . Finally

Saturday, April 8, 1911 "Her ultimate freedom . . . may still be a matter of from one to two weeks," stated *The New York Times*. "Little fear of her safety in the meantime is felt. The only note of uncertainty on this point was sounded early this morning by M.L. Dunbar, one of the United States Coast Inspectors. The wind was then blowing from the northeast. Inspector Dunbar pointed out that such a wind would tend to churn up the waters under the *Irene*'s bow, causing the sand there to shift, thus leaving both stern and bow clear, with the vessel's beam resting on the imprisoning sand bar. The British tramp steamer, *Drumelsie*," the *Times* continued, "which grounded off Point o' Woods in a similar position three years ago, buckled and broke up in the middle."

The discrepancy over the outcome of the *Prinzess Irene*'s grounding continued as the hours passed. Several experienced seamen and tug boat captains offered their opinions that she would remain in the sand another week.

"I've seen many a steamboat stuck in the sand, and it'll be quite some time before this lassy's loose."

"A-up, she's sure to stay for a good many days."

6:00 A.M. The *Prinz Friedrich Wilhelm*, which had left Robbin's Reef at 1:00 A.M., approached its pier at Hoboken where the passengers were to be taken to Ellis Island. A deafening drone of indecipherable babble arose among the passengers as they drew closer and closer to the dock.

"What ever is the matter with them?" a crewman hollered to another. "Just a minute ago they were as quiet as mice."

"I don't know. But we'd better go and see."

Upon discovery, the crewmen were wide-eyed as they watched the passengers before them. Men were yelling and hollering, women and children were screaming and grabbing bundles and valises from each others' hands. It was chaos, and the men ran forward as more crewmen arrived to separate the mob. The male passengers were very determined, and it was several minutes before things were quiet again.

"And what is the meaning of this," one crewman asked.

A bilingual passenger stepped forward and spoke up.

"They're afraid their luggage is going to get mixed up," he explained. "The steerage passengers don't want the cabin passengers to walk away with their valises."

A few of the crewmen swapped glances. Around them men, women and children clung to tightly wrapped bundles, stuffed valises and manageable chests or boxes.

"Pfff, they all look the same to me," said one crewman as his eyes scanned the brightly colored material and decorated cardboard. "How do they know which is theirs anyhow?" A baby's cry suddenly rang out before a reply could be made, and a woman dashed to one of her children and took a particular bundle into her own arms.

"A babe's wrapped in there?" one of the crewman laughed.

"It could have been a wad of clothing, for all I know," laughed the first, then he turned back to the bilingual passenger. "Why don't you tell these people that nobody's going to lose their luggage, okay? I've been doing this whole immigrant thing for years, and nobody's ever come up to me and complained about losing their luggage."

The passenger turned toward the immigrants and translated the news, though it was questionable whether they believed the crewman or not. The *New York Times* would later report that the passengers' concern for their smaller luggage, bundles and valises was so great that many of the immigrants were seen sleeping on them ever since the *Prinzess Irene* had grounded.

Back at work, the crewmen prepared for docking the liner. As the boat slowed, the crewmen lowered the gangplank, and called for the disembarkment. The 235 cabin passengers went first. The 1,485 steerage passengers remained on deck until about noon, waiting for the rest of their luggage to be brought from the *Prinzess Irene*.

"Not one ounce of displeasure," remarked a *New York Times* newspaper reporter. He was standing to the side as the passengers left the *Prinz Friedrich Wilhelm*. "No frowns, no fear, no complaints."

"Nope, they're just as happy and as lighthearted as if they just returned from a pleasure trip."

At Ellis Island, more examinations and immigration requirements awaited the passengers. Nations and tongues mingled as hundreds of immigrants packed together. Each individual moved ahead to face the officer, knowing that their immigrant acceptance sat squarely in his hands. He could deem them too ill to stay, or admit them to the hospital or, as everyone hoped, could bang his stamp of approval on their passport. His stern features hid any hint of emotion.

It was different when the Marones stepped up, though.

"Ha, de wife has anodder babee every trip home, eh? Hey fellas, take a peek at diss . . ."

The stern look was swept right off the officer's face, and replaced with hearty laughter as he glanced at Raffaele's travel records. His gaze also fell on the line of children that stood behind Raffaele and Rosa.

Raffaele laughed too, and engaged in a bit of conversation as the officer stamped the seven passports. Rosa and the girls waited quietly, wondering about the laughter and excited conversation. The distraction, however, didn't keep their eyes and ears from being peeled for the activities around them. They were in a new country now, where the sights and sounds were strange and sometimes scary.

"And what was so funny back there?" said Rosa when they had finally passed the necessary exams, tests, questionings and routines. "It was a joke on me, wasn't it?"

"No, it wasn't on you," laughed Raffaele. "He just thought it was comical that you had a child after each of my visits home."

Rosa laughed too, this time with the older girls joining in.

"And as we speak," she whispered, "we are expecting yet another one."

12 o' clock noon Back at the *Prinzess Irene* Captain Peterssen was busy sending a wireless telegram to Oelrichs & Co., the agents for North German Lloyd liners. He asked that lighters* be sent to take the cargo off the *Prinzess Irene*. "Her current position is most favorable," he added.

There was a high wind, but Captain Peterssen did not feel his liner was in danger. His cargo was light, mainly Italian merchandise packaged in small sizes, amounting to 2,780 tons of macaroni, spaghetti, silk, lemons, cheese, talc, wines, currants, olive oil and straw goods.

Oelrichs & Co. responded to Captain Peterssen's request by sending a lighter. It arrived at the *Prinzess Irene* near 1 P.M., and went away two hours later loaded with cargo. A second lighter didn't arrive until 4:20 P.M. and it quickly became apparent that it would be several days before the *Prinzess Irene*'s cargo would be completely unloaded. The cargo not only needed to get ashore, but the lessened weight would greatly assist in dislodging the *Prinzess Irene*.

"As the weight of the *Prinzess Irene* decreases," proclaimed the *New York Times*, "more efforts will be made to dislodge her from the sand ... waiting in the water nearby are the *A.J. Merritt*, the *Mohawk* and the *Seneca*, along with the *Rescue*, which was sent from Norfolk this morning."

On the beach of Fire Island, the onlookers continued to watch and wait. Watching to see what steps would be taken to move the liner, and waiting for it all to happen. Besides the hundreds of spectators from Sayville, lifesavers from the Lone Hill and the Point o' Woods stations patrolled the beach, even though their assistance was determined unnecessary earlier in the day. When they finally left, they took the breeches buoy with them.

While the possible causes of the grounding were numerous,

the lifesavers, sailors and other sea officials rarely voiced their personal opinions.

"Many factors have certainly played a part in the grounding..." said a seaman slowly, choosing his words carefully.

"But we all know that Captain Peterssen frankly and undeniably lost his way," another boldly interjected. "And I think that those currents along the Long Island shore, which can be treacherous when certain tidal conditions are present, should definitely be considered."

Before the day came to a close, Coast Inspector Albert Ketcham, of Inwood, went aboard the *Prinzess Irene* to speak with Captain Peterssen. Captain Peterssen's worry for his ship and confusion over the grounding could not be hidden from the Inspector. Perhaps it was the stress that compelled Captain Peterssen to disallow further *New York Times* reporters aboard his liner, but the men's conversation was later relayed to those on shore when the Inspector returned in his small boat.

"From the way things are, it appears to me that you steered fully one-half point too far north after you left Nantucket Lightship."

Captain Peterssen was too confused to fully follow, but listened closely as the Inspector continued.

"At that point, you were 377 miles from Sandy Hook and probably got your bearings at six o'clock on... Tuesday morning, is that right?" Captain Peterssen nodded and continued to listen. "There you should have laid your course north..."

"And that's exactly what I did, sir," Captain Peterssen interrupted.

"Uh-huh, but you see, by steering too far north, your vessel had gone nearly ten miles out of her course."

When Albert Ketcham had left, Captain Peterssen wasn't feeling much better. He turned away as the Inspector dropped out of his vision as crewmen lowered the davit drops.

Back on shore, Albert Ketcham was greeted by Peter Ritter, a United Stated Coast Guard surveyor, who had been given orders by the Coast Survey to keep an eye on the *Prinzess Irene* situation. He had measured off the distances to chart the precise location of the stranded liner, and was just finishing when Albert Ketcham rowed in.

"She's 3,994 feet from the flagstaff of the Lone Hill Life Saving Station," he reported, "and 364 yards from the high water line on the beach."

Palm Sunday, April 9, 1911 Onlookers, determined to watch every move involved with the *Prinzess Irene*, continued to crowd the Fire Island beach. They seemed to believe that watching the incident at sea was more interesting than going to church or returning home for traditions or celebrations. The continued high winds and rough seas seemed to laugh at the plan to dislodge the *Prinzess Irene*.

* *Lighter*: Commonly an unpowered, flat-bottomed barge, used in lightening, unloading, loading or transporting goods for short distances.

CHAPTER SEVENTEEN

How It Happened

The final leg of the Marones' journey was at hand. It had been nearly two weeks since they had left their home in Laurenzana and the thought of putting the traveling behind them was satisfying.

"Well, here's home," Raffaele offered. His extended finger pointed towards a street sign above their heads. "Twenty-sixth Second Avenue."

"On the street, Papa?" said one of the girls. She turned quickly at a passerby. The minute they had left Ellis Island, Rosa and the girls had been wary of this new place. The sights of women in strangely styled dresses, make-up and broad rimmed hats were worth staring at while the loud noises, city sites, large crowds that spoke indecipherable words were a thing to be feared.

"No, no, no," he smiled. He could sense his family's confidence in him as their dark eyes darted all around them and as they hung close to him as the family walked. "We go inside over there." Raffaele pointed once more down the sidewalk as he led his family to a side door. Out from under the sun, the building was dark and cool. Up the stairs, around corners, past the doors. An occasional window lit the indoors with a murky dimness.

"Our apartment is this one right here," Raffale said finally. They had walked the length of the building, and stood together as he unlocked the door and swung it open, revealing to his wife and children what would be their home for the next six years.

The girls scurried inside, anxious to unload their arms. They left their *madre* standing just inside the door and ran in different directions through the apartment. Rosa stood with her arms still loaded, her keen eye taking in the floors, the ceilings and the walls.

These rooms could sure use a good cleaning, she thought to herself.

She scuffed her shoe across the floor and wondered how long it had been since a broom had been used. She sighed, unaware of her husband's eyes watching her responding moves.

I wonder what life in The Bronx would have been like. Ha, married to a Chocolate Factory man? Rosa shook off the thought as she turned her attention to the rest of the family.

"And this is the second bedroom," Raffaele was saying. When Rosa turned her attention to him, he had looked the other way and was now absorbing himself in his daughters as they trailed behind him. "And last of all, this is the kitchen. When you have to go to the bathroom, it's out in the hallway where I showed you before. Oh, I almost forgot. That window over there will show you the courtyard that's out back. Go take a look."

The girls darted across the empty room and looked out at a large, cold-looking building. Far below, they could see a wide opened courtyard.

"That building you see," Raffaele explained over their shoulders, "is a prison house."

A few of the girls gasped, and Michaelina turned from the window. "The bad guys won't come out and get us, right Papa?"

"Oh no, they have to stay behind the bars. See there," pointed Raffaele, "those strong bars at the windows will keep them in and you out." He quietly turned and walked off to find his wife, while conversation about the bad men in jail formed among the girls at the window.

"I'm going to step out for just a minute, dear. I'll be back soon . . ."

It was late, and Rosa and the girls were too tired to do more than prepare for bed. They left their valises packed and the other packaged items undisturbed. They only wanted a good night's rest. The voices down on the streets, the footsteps from other tenement occupants, the distant cracks and booms blurred together in their dreams.

"Papa, I heard loud noises last night," said Donatine. The family was eating their first breakfast in their new home, and remnants of their belongings scattered the room. Rosa had gotten up early and had begun dispersing their small pile of things among the three rooms.

"Mmm?" replied Raffaele. "Don't worry, just the sounds of the city. You'll get used to them soon."

"I heard them too, Papa," said Michaelina. "They were loud booms."

"Oh," said Raffaele, waving his hand through the air. "That would be the Maffia. They . . ."

"Maffia? What's that?" asked Maria.

"Italians. They aren't happy with the laws here, and try to make people listen to them. What you heard last night was probably just a couple of bombs. But don't worry about it . . ."

Rosa was listening carefully. *Don't worry?* She raised her eyebrows.

"What does that say, Papa?" asked Maria as she pointed towards the newspaper that Raffaele had picked up. Bold black letters ran across the top of the page and smaller ones filled the rest in slender columns. "And what does that say?" she added before he had the opportunity to answer her first question.

"This over here," pointed Raffaele, "says, 'Liner *Irene* Afloat And Not Much Hurt: Freed from Grip of the Sand Bar That Held Her Prisoner on Fire Island 83 Hours.'" Raffaele was fluent in English, and he translated what he was reading into Italian.

"And this over here," continued Raffaele, "says, 'Will Reach Her Pier Today; Waiting for Daylight to be Towed Through Ambrose Channel—Rudder Post Damaged—Not Leaking.'"

The girls stared at the undecipherable words that filled the page. The pictures were much more interesting, and they turned their attention to them.

"There's the *Prinzess Irene*," observed Grazia as she pointed to a picture the reporters had taken.

"And this was when we were getting rescued," Maria pointed out with big eyes. The grounding and transfer had made such an impression on them that they were still awestruck.

"Mmm-hmm," acknowledged Raffaele. "Do you want me to read the story to you?" He turned the pages back to the beginning of the article.

"Yes, please do Papa."

Raffaele skipped down past the printed date of Sunday, April 9, 1911 and other peripheral information. "Okay, let's see. Ah ha, here's where the story starts. 'At six o'clock this morning lifesaver Bill Reynolds, returning from patrol to the Lone Hill Station, reported that there was a bad north-northeast storm starting, with the wind between twenty and twenty-five miles an hour. In the night there had been rain, which bade fair to whip down the expected rise of sea due with the strong southeast wind of Saturday afternoon and night. The rain, however, soon changed to hail, and later snow, which was driving viciously at 6 A.M., covering the sand dunes with a depth of three inches. There was snow on the superstructure of the *Irene*, too.

"'At high tide at 4 A.M., the wrecking tugs had made another attempt to loosen her. The lead line dropped from her stern showed that they budged her only slightly. The effect of the sea wind from the southeast, however, continued long after the blow had veered shoreward, the sea piling up around the ship and running high nearly all day. It was expected to reach its crest at 3 o'clock in the afternoon . . .'"

A yell from the streets below suddenly disrupted the girls' attention.

"What was that?" gasped Maria.

"Just someone calling to their friend," assured Raffaele.

"'The surf meanwhile was rolling in high from the southeast,'" he continued. "'It broke so hard and so high that, taut under the strain of the strong shore blow, the thin rope which the lifesavers had stretched again from the ship to the breeches buoy late Saturday night parted with an angry snap soon after midnight.

"'Captain Baker of Point o' Woods and Captain Goddard of the Lone Hill Life Saving Station held a long consultation on the beach at 10 o'clock in the morning, as to whether they should stretch another lifeline to the ship. They finally decided that the surf was too high to risk launching a lifeboat. The crest of the surf rollers brimmed up to the *Irene*'s tier of lower deadlights.

"'A crowd of about 200 persons had gathered on the beach at noon, gay and frolicking as holiday picnickers, to look at the discomfited liner. At 1 o'clock in the afternoon the tugs *Relief* and *Rescue* nosed their way about 200 feet astern of the *Irene*, the former southeast, on her starboard, and the latter at a similar position to port, and began to tug at the hawsers they had thrown upon the liner.

"'Just about this time Captain Goddard, who has hobnobbed half the century with the sea . . .'"

"What does 'hobnob' mean?" said Maria.

Rosa could see Raffaele's patience being stretched, so she replied, "What they mean is that Captain Goddard has had lots of experience in dealing with the ocean. He's a very wise man when it comes to ships and the sea." She nodded to Raffaele, and he continued.

"Now, where were we? Oh yes, 'Capt. Goddard, who has hobnobbed half a century with the sea . . .'"

"How much is a half a century?" asked Michaelina.

Rosa chuckled as Raffaele dropped the paper into his lap and sighed, "How many more questions are you going ask? Can't you just listen to me read?"

"Dear, they are just trying to understand." Rosa's soothing tone did not seem to do much for the patience that her husband lacked. She was still smiling when he picked the paper back up. "And," she added, "a half a century is fifty years."

"Now for the third time, 'Capt. Goddard, who had hobnobbed half a century with the sea—calm and angry and indifferent—along Fire Island, and knows it like a brother, tugged his blue cap over his blue eyes and his gray moustachios to starboard and to port, announced to his men: 'Well, boys, I expect I'll go to the station. They won't loosen that old woman for a week or so, I guess.' And with a deprecating shrug to the tugs, he went.

"'A few of the lifesavers remained, lounging about a large bonfire near the beach cart and around these gathered a fast-growing crowd of shore folk. Other groups lay scattered about the beach, from which the snow, which stopped falling at about 7 o'clock, had now almost melted away. Suddenly at two thirty o'clock, a few persons on the beach cried out that the *Irene* was rocking. Sure enough, under the steady pull of the two tugs that were bucking their bows into her rollers astern of her, the masts of the *Irene* could be seen wobbling now to port, now to starboard, and a few moments later it was seen that the vessel's stern, too, was swinging slowly from side to side. Evidently the grip of the sandbar was loosening in the high sea about her.

"'At 2:50 P.M. in the afternoon, with both tugs still pulling at the same angle at either side astern, the *Irene*'s bow was seen to rise slowly. Even there the sand was losing its hold. A few of the lifesavers, confident in the judgement of their old seabarking Captain, still declared cheerfully, "she'd stick" for all of six or seven days, tugs or no tugs. A few minutes later, the little tugs *John J. Timmons* and *John Nichols* swung across the *Irene*'s bow ashore of her, and began to shove her, with their little noses against her huge steel bulk.'"

"Is that the end?" asked Maria.

Raffaele impatiently scanned the next page and shook his head. "It says here that 'at 3:03 o'clock, the *Irene*'s sea anchor cables began to slacken, showing that she was really backing, loose and free . . .'"

"Hurrah! Hurrah!" cheered the younger girls.

"There's more. 'Slowly her kedge anchors* were hoisted aboard. There was a gathering roar of hurrahs all along the beach, in which the cheers of the lifesavers were given with just as much gusto as if they hadn't been preluded with a surprised half-whispered chorus of: 'By gosh! She's loose.'

"'The *Irene*, free at last, replied to the cheers ashore with two long blasts of her siren, and moved in tow of the tugs slowly out to sea. At 4 o'clock, still towed by the *Relief* and *Rescue*, and with the *Timmons* astern, the *Irene* was standing about a mile off shore, just opposite the Lone Hill Life Saving Station, in the lookout of which Captain Goddard gazed skeptically through his telescope, muttering again and again and yet once again that he sure would 'be blowed'—a windy fate that is sure to beset Captain Goddard almost any day, whether he will it or no. He said later that even if he was surprised, he was pleased, too; and well he might be, for he and his men worked untiringly.

"'When the *Irene* turned westward on the last lap of her interrupted journey she ran down the red signal, which spelled 'Haul away on your cables,' and ran up the German ensign. The crowd on shore broke into cheers.'"

"Why did he say to haul away on your cables?"

"Captain Peterssen wanted all the newspaper reporters to go ahead and tell the story in their papers," said Rosa.

Raffaele continued. "'A little later, when the vessel was well under way, her skipper wirelessed to the line's office, the best message he ever sent there: 'The *Prinzess Irene* is free, and is being towed by tugs *Rescue* and *Relief*. She is undamaged . . .'"

"But it said before that she was damaged," corrected Maria.

"Yes, dear," said Rosa, "but a damaged rudder post is probably considered to be minor."

"'With the departure of the *Irene* and her rescuing tugs, there remained at the scene of the stranding only the Government revenue cutter *Mohawk*. The derelict destroyer *Seneca*, which had stood by the grounded *Irene* from the start, having departed earlier in the day, presumably to hunt a derelict she had heard of further east.

"'Some of those in the crowd of holiday spectators, hovered about the beach until darkness was settling and the *Irene* had become a mere toy ship on the western horizon. The rest trudged back across Fire Island to Great South Bay, where thrifty boatmen who, for three days had found passenger ferrying much more lucrative than oyster dredging, slung them one by one upon their back, and carried them, with their feet dangling just clear of the water, to waiting flat-bottomed doreys and thereon out to waiting motor boats, oyster boats and sailboats, further out in the bay. It was night when the last of them reached Sayville. Sayville went to bed at 9:30 instead of 9 o'clock last night, all through talking of the launching of the *Irene*.'"

"Is that the end?" asked Maria as Raffaele closed and folded the paper.

"It's the end of the story in yesterday's paper. But . . ." he said as he left his chair. "I picked up today's paper this morning before you got up, and the rest of the story is in here."

* *Kedge anchor:* Used in kedging, the process of moving a ship by means of a line that is attached to a small anchor dropped at the distance, and in the direction, desired. The vessel is then hauled toward the anchor where the process is repeated until the desired destination is reached.

CHAPTER EIGHTEEN

How It Ended

"The headlines say 'Now Rides At Anchor; *Prinzess Irene* Will Come Through the Ambrose Channel This Morning,'" said Raffaele. He pointed at the words printed across the newspaper page and then followed more words farther down on the page. "Here's where the rest of the story begins. 'The *Prinzess Irene* anchored off Scotland Lightship at 10 o'clock last night, waiting for daylight to be towed through the Ambrose Channel and the bay to her pier at Hoboken, which she will reach at 10 a.m.

"'When the liner got into deep water from the sand bar, where she had rested for eighty-three hours, Chief Engineer Schmidt examined the machinery and reported to Captain von Peterssen that, so far as he could see, there was no reason why the ship should not proceed slowly under her own steam up the harbor. After a consultation between the Captain, Chief Engineer and the Inspector Koevenick, from Hoboken, it was decided that as the wrecking people had reported that the rudder post appeared to be damaged, it would be advisable not to use the propellers, and the two tugs then started to tow her along at three knots an hour. She was not leaking, and there was no sign to show that the hull had been damaged during the time she was ashore.

"'The North German Lloyd officials said yesterday that when the liner arrives at her pier divers will go down and examine her hull to see if any of the plates have been started, and then she will proceed to Newport News under her own steam, if possible, to go into dry dock for necessary repairs.

"'The *Prinzess Irene* was to have sailed next Saturday for Naples, and had 160 first and 100 second class cabin passengers who have been notified of her inability to leave on schedule time. The next North German Lloyd vessel to leave for the Mediterranean is the *Koenig Albert* on April 29, and if she arrives in New York in time her sailing date will be advanced, it was said, and the *Prinzess Irene* will take her place.

"'Officals of the company and the seafaring friends of Captain Peterssen said last night that the ship having got off safely, with comparatively little damage, they hoped that he would not lose his position in the service, as it was his first accident during a long career, which included eleven years in command. So far everything went to prove that he had done his duty as navigator and a commander in time of emergency.

"'Captain Moeller, formerly commander of one of the company's South American liners and for several years the Marine Superintendent, of the North German Lloyd at Hoboken, was sick in bed when the *Prinzess Irene* went ashore on Thursday, and in order to be in touch with the ship he had a telephone line hooked up beside his bed so that he could get the reports coming in from Inspector Koevenick, his assistant, who went on board the stranded liner.

"'It was stated that 200 tons out of her general cargo of 900 tons was discharged from the *Prinzess Irene* before she was floated.'"

"Nine hundred tons? That's this big," exclaimed Michaelina with out stretched arms. Her eyes were wide.

"No, no," corrected Maria. "Nine hundred tons is much bigger than that. You couldn't even lift nine hundred tons."

"Yes, I could," insisted Michaelina.

"No, you couldn't!"

"Yes, I could!"

"Girls, girls! That's enough," scolded Rosa. "Now come over here and help me fix dinner."

* * *

"'We left Gibraltar on Monday, March 27, at 6:05 P.M.,'" read Raffaele in a low voice, the interview that the *New York Times* reporters had printed lay before him on the table, "'and had rough weather to the Azores with west northwest winds.'" The girls were off to bed, and Rosa listened as Captain von Letten Peterssen told the story in his own words.

"'On April 3 there was very stormy weather, with a twenty-five mile north northwest wind. On Tuesday, April 4, it was so hazy at noon I could not take an observation by the sun. I managed, however, to get a [star] at 6:50 o'clock that night, which was the last observation I made. From that time, until we struck on the bar at 3:55 yesterday morning, our course was laid by dead reckoning. The position of the ship, as I made it from the observations taken by the star, was latitude 29:24 north and longitude 63 west.

"'On Wednesday,'" continued Raffaele, translating for his wife as he went along, "'April 5, the weather at noon was very hazy with light rains and I could not see the horizon. I had soundings taken every hour, beginning at noon that day and found that they compared with those taken on the previous voyage in clear weather.

"'At 8 o'clock that night we ran into a heavy fog and reduced our speed to four knots, just enough to keep steerage way on the ship. All the watertight bulkheads were closed as usual when the first blast of the fog horn sounded and they were kept shut until we went aground.

"'The soundings were taken all through the night every hour, and there was nothing to indicate that we were running into the land. At 2 a.m. yesterday I was on the bridge with Second Officer Hoennecke and Fourth Officer Vessering. There was a lookout in the bows and one in the crow's nest. The fog lifted then, and I told the lookout forward to go into the crow's nest with the other man and keep his eyes open for the Fire Island Lightship.

"'Going by the soundings I judged that the ship was fifteen miles to the south of the lightship. I laid the course five degrees to the north and allowed two degrees for drifting, and believed that we should pass seven miles south of the lightship.

"'A few minutes after four bells [two o'clock] I gave the order to go full speed ahead, which is fourteen knots an hour. The horizon was clear four or five miles ahead. At 3:30 I was on the bridge and could not see any land. The ship was drawing 22 feet aft and 19 ½ feet forward. Suddenly, at 3:55 o'clock, I felt a shock as her keel went over the bar, and I knew that we were aground. I stopped the engines and then went full speed astern immediately in hope of getting her off, but she did not move.

"'The deadlights were lowered over the ports on the steerage deck so that the immigrants could not be alarmed at seeing land at hand when daylight came, and also in case of danger of the water coming in. The ballast tanks were pumped out, and I had the ship listed over to 45 degrees. With the aid of one good tug I could have got her off but the wind rose and blew at the rate of twenty-four miles an hour from the southwest, which set her up again on an even keel. Captain Peterssen added that he had been eleven years in command of North German Lloyd liners in China, Australia, Argentine, and the Atlantic trade. This is his fourth year as Captain of the *Prinzess Irene*, and he has never had an accident before.'"

"Hmm, that was quite interesting. I hope Captain Peterssen's career won't be ruined, don't you?"

Raffaele had flipped a few pages of the paper and had begun to read another article silently to himself. He started, "What, dear?"

"I was just saying how I hoped Captain Peterssen's career doesn't get ruined on account of the grounding."

"No, no I don't think it would. I mean, he's a very experienced and successful seaman. I don't think the North German Lloyd Company would want to lose someone like him."

Rosa nodded her head in agreement. Raffaele returned to the article he was reading and Rosa finished the hem she was sewing. A while longer, she yawned.

"Why don't you get off to bed?" suggested Raffaele, glancing at his wife.

"I think I will," she said, yawning again. She moaned as she pulled her tired, pregnant body into the standing position. "*Buona notte*.*"

"*Buona notte, Rosa, chi bella Rosa.*"

---

*   *Buona notte (bwona' notte):* goodnight

CHAPTER NINETEEN

Life in America

"*Buon giorno*"! Oh, excuse us sir, pardon me, miss." Rosa chattered her way through the streets of New York with her daughters in tow. The first months in New York had passed quickly, the strangeness of a new place had dissipated and the once uncanny sights and sounds become familiar.

Swinging the basket of purchased items, Rosa took a deep breath. "Oh, isn't it a beautiful day?"

"Yes, it surely is," replied a newfound friend in quick Italian. "I'll be glad when I can clean out the house and get some fresh air in there." The women laughed. "With seven children, it sure gets stuffy in there."

Rosa glanced at her own clan, and shook her head. "I guess I can't complain about my five, can I? And you've been here three years, did you say?"

"Yes, it was three years just last month. My husband says we'll be leaving soon, and I honestly can't wait. I'd give anything to be able to sit in the long grass again, or walk through a big open field."

Spring was giving way to summer, creating a delightful atmosphere for the Marones' new baby. Back at the apartment, Rosa and the girls were spring cleaning, making the space, limited as it was, clean and welcoming.

"Michaelina and Donatine, take these linens outdoors and shake them out, please," Rosa said. "And Maria, you can clean the windows. Here's a rag to use." Windows open, the sparse furniture moved, linens aired and washed and all in time for the new baby.

101

He arrived on July 26, 1911 and was named Antonio, after his grandfather.

"Ah, a son," the doctor smiled at Raffaele.

"Finally!"

Back in Laurenzana, the wheat would have just been harvested, the grass a deep green, the flowers in full bloom. Antonio's birth was surrounded instead by nothing more than the busy city streets and the tall tenement houses of New York City. The oddity of a baby boy in the house was strange at first, but the girls soon began to hold and tend him as they would have another girl. Antonio grew quickly as Rosa recovered and returned to life as a new mother.

On hot afternoons in late summer, she found herself shooing her daughters out to play.

"Go on now, it's much too stuffy in here for you to be closed in all day. Enjoy the fresh air, and don't get into trouble." The city air left a certain longing for the fresh country air of Italy and the open windows only seemed to beckon more of the stale air.

"Yes, Mama..." The girls opened the door and turned from the apartment.

"And be sure to stay together. Don't get your dresses dirty, and mind you stay out of Chinatown." The girls' feet could be heard clattering down the dimly lit halls. "Those Chinamen will chop you up and you won't come home any more. And don't go to the park..."

Alone with Antonio, Rosa would rest her head back and close her eyes. She would dream about her mother, her father, her brother. She would dream about Laurenzana. Visions of rolling hills and wide open village terrain would rush to her mind and she could almost feel the comfortable breeze blowing wisps of her hair. She could see the green hills and distant mountains standing against a deep blue sky. Villagers on their way home would stop to share an afternoon chat. Her children could run and play in the swaying grass or walk to their *nonno*'s house. The large fields and small village allowed the girls to run free with the sheep dogs.

Little did Rosa know that the streets below offered her daughters an entirely different atmosphere than the hills of Laurenzana, and a whole new realm of things to do. What Rosa assumed to be a pleasurable walk down the street, the girls transformed into rowdy games. Filled with the energy that had been suppressed by weeks and months in the apartment, the girls let themselves loose.

"This way, follow me," Grazia would gesture.

Of course, Giovanna and the others would follow, led by the desire that dwells in the heart of every youngster to explore, free from all restraint. Their lives virtually void of toys, save a jumping rope or two, the girls made a playground out of the city and its streets. Down an alley and around a corner, under a stairway and beyond the crowds. Every day provided a new destination to reach or a new hideout to discover.

"You chase me, and try to catch me before I reach the top. Ready, go." The tenement fire escapes proved to be lots of fun, and when storm clouds gathered, or the sun shone too bright, the cool dimness was welcoming.

"Let's play that game, oh what is it called?" said Grazia one day.

"Do you mean that one they taught us at school the other day?" The girls were standing in the courtyard behind the tenement, enjoying the breeze and sun. "It was something 'Scotch' . . ."

"H-h . . ."

"That's right, it was Hop Scotch. Here, let's show Michaelina and Donatine how to play."

As the older girls gave directions and explained the game, a group of onlookers was watching their every move. They watched as the girls collected a few rocks and sticks, which they used to make the lines and numbers for the game. Soon, the game was underway and the girls were laughing and enjoying the sport.

"Hey down there," one of the onlookers suddenly hollered.

In return, the girls screamed and dashed out of sight.

"Quick, run for your lives. Hurry, hurry!" But while the girls' heels were hitting their backs, their pursuers were not advancing. Throwing themselves in the shadows of some old barrels, the girls caught their breath. "Was it a bad guy?" said Donatine.

Grazia was determined to quench all fear, and shook her head vigorously.

"You don't know that," whispered Michaelina. "It could have been a bad guy. We were playing right next to the jailhouse, remember." Her eyes grew big.

The next few minutes passed in silence between the girls. They listened for footsteps or voices, but they heard nothing.

"Let's get back out," suggested Maria.

"Wait, we have to have a plan first," said Grazia.

"I think we should just get out of here," suggested Giovanna, her eyes overflowing with fear.

"Nah, I think we should . . ."

"We have to have a plan," Grazia repeated. Several more minutes passed as the girls whispered their thoughts and opinions.

* *Buon giorno (bwon' d/orno):* good morning

CHAPTER TWENTY

Progress

"Giovanna, it's your turn now. Here's the stone." The girls were back in the courtyard, and while they were fully enjoying the competition and entertainment, they were keeping half an eye on the activities around them. Giovanna tossed the stone, and hopped through the squares in the acclaimed order. Then Maria took a turn, then Michaelina, then Donatine. The cycle went round and round.

Suddenly, when they were least expecting it, the dreaded holler echoed through the courtyard. "Hey, down there," someone called, their voice big and terrible and scary.

This time, instead of running into oblivion and dashing into safety, the girls stayed put. They turned in their tracks and craned their necks.

"I don't see anyone, do you?" Maria asked in a hushed voice.

"No," replied the others. There were plenty of passers-by, shoppers, children and old ladies out for a walk. But no one had stopped to talk.

"This is too weird," said Grazia. "Come on, let's just pretend we don't hear it next time." She turned back to the game and the others followed. This time, Maria had only begun to toss the stone, when the holler came the third time.

"Hey you, down there, I'm up here." With that, the girls looked up, and up and up. Almost directly above them a man's face could just barely be seen protruding from the jailhouse bars. "Hey down there."

The girls looked at each other, and stepped back across the courtyard, for a better view and to create as much distance as they could.

"We're just playing a game here, mister," said Michaelina. "We aren't doing anything wrong."

But the jailbird wasn't assuming such. "I just wanted to make friends. You're nice little girls, wouldn't you like some money?" As he spoke, his hands were moving busily behind the bars. As he finished speaking, he let out a long string from the window. "Ah, too short."

"No, we don't want any of your money," Grazia called back. Under her breath she turned to her sisters. "He probably stole it, for all we know."

"Not for you, my missies. Ha, ha, for me! I want you to take my money and buy something for me, for me. Not for you, for me." His laughter brought other jailbirds to their windows, and soon several scruffy faces were peering down at the girls.

"Ya, ya, buy me something too," they called, and began throwing coins into the courtyard. Donatine and Michaelina scurried in different directions to pick them up. "Ha, ha," the men bellowed, "cigarettes, cigarettes. Go on, and bring us back some cigarettes." The men were happier when, quite a while later, the girls returned.

"We can't throw the cigarettes up there, the windows are too high," Giovanna puzzled. "Hmm . . ."

"I know," one of the others suggested, "Those barrels we hid behind. Those would work."

"Ah ha . . ."

Soon, with one barrel stacked on another, the girls were passing up a cigarette at a time to their new-found friends. Newfound friends that Rosa or Raffaele might not have been too excited about, but whom the girls found to be quite pleasant.

The passing months found Rosa and the girls becoming more and more acquainted with American life. The older girls had become enrolled in school, and their first Christmas had come and gone. As much as they still spoke Italian and lived their lives in Italian ways, the Marones were being pulled into American life by tides stronger than they could fight against. At school, the girls had been given Americanized names, introduced to English and expected to emulate American manners.

"Grazia, we'll call you Grace. And Giovanna, that name's rather difficult to say, so you can be called Jennie. Now Maria, that's just the same as Mary . . ."

The Catholic nuns seemed indifferent to cutting the girls' ties to the old country, and shooed them off to play without a second thought to the humiliation that resulted in their changed identity.

Out in the school yard, the girls were grouped with strangers and called to play games they didn't understand. They no doubt rejoiced, however, that they could keep each other company in the midst of the unfamiliarity and strangeness.

"Let's go play on the fire escapes," one of them would suggest. At home, the tenement fire escapes had proven to be fun, and the similarity between the two offered a sense of familiarity. After long days of being "Americanized," home was a place where the girls could return to their "Italy" and dive into conversation using the familiar tongue and antics. It was a place where strange manners and expectations could be forgotten and where traditions and rituals from their homeland could be recalled.

"*Ciao**, Mama! We're home!" the girls cried as they arrived from school one afternoon. They quickly entered the dim apartment, lit only by the firelight from the stove. Their shoes were caked with snow and flakes topped their shoulders and sleeves.

"Cold out there?" asked Rosa, noticing the red noses and cheeks. She was sitting on the floor amid scraps of material.

"Yes, very," breathed Grazia, then took a deep breath. "Mmm, dinner smells so wonderful." She finished taking off her winter garb, and walked toward the table. Giovanna and Maria soon joined her and they each took a thick slice of warm bread.

"Maria, guess what the puppy did while you were gone?" said Michaelina with a grin. She and Donatine lifted their hands to their mouths to keep from exploding with laughter.

Maria glanced toward the corner of the room where the family puppy, which the girls had found and taken in after begging their parents' permission, lay. "I don't know," she said finally. "Tell me."

"He ate my dress," Michaelina blurted with laughter. She began to clap and jiggle up and down, chanting, "Hurrah, hurrah, I can wear *regular* clothes all the time now."

"And he chewed my shoe," wailed Donatine.

The older girls joined the laughter.

"Girls, please," Rosa hollered above the chaos. "Donatine, Michaelina, couldn't you just stand still for a few more minutes? I just have the sleeves left to pin." Her eyes begged with her daughters, though their faces pleaded innocent. "Now, just hold your arms like this," guided Rosa. She reached for another pin. "I'm almost through."

"There," Rosa finally ejaculated. The sigh she emitted turned into a grunt as she gathered her skirts and stood up. "Now put your other clothes back on, please. And remember to be quiet; Antonio needs his nap."

Rosa sat down in a chair near the firelight and began to sew the new dresses, talking with her daughters about their day at school. She squinted to see her stitches as her needle flashed reflections of the flames. Suddenly, a loud boom interrupted their conversation, and every item in the room shook for several seconds.

*   *Ciao ('t /ao):* hi, hello

CHAPTER TWENTY-ONE

Hello . . . Goodbye

The girls screamed loudly. Rosa joined them, dropping her sewing onto the floor. Soon, they were all gathered together in the center of the room, in a close huddle. It was all over rather quickly, but Rosa shuddered even so.

"Tsk, tsk, that'll be the baby," said Rosa as a wail reached her ears. But before she could leave her chair, a knock on the apartment door interrupted her.

"Papa?" asked one of the girls.

"No," Rosa smiled weakly, "much too early for your *padre*." She walked to the door, calling over her shoulder, "Grazia, go and get Antonio, please." At the door, Rosa opened it a small crack, and then stepped back as she beckoned fervently. "Oh, come in. Hurry."

"Ugh! The Maffia," scoffed the friend with emotion as she slipped through the door. "So very terrible."

"Are you all right? You weren't hurt, were you?"

"No, I'm fine. I was already in the building when they bombed."

The girls listened as the women conversed, Rosa finally sweeping her hand through the air as if to remove the events of the day from her mind. She moved her sewing scraps off the table and pulled up a second chair. "Here, we can sit right here at the table."

"Ah, but isn't it kind of dark?" said Rosa's friend. She was eyeing a gas lamp nearby.

Rosa sighed as she joined her friend at the table. The girls could see a mix of embarrassment in their *madre*'s eyes as she confessed. "I'm frightened of that lamp. We usually sit here in the dark until the girls bring my husband home from work . . ."

"Oh . . ."

"But we can get a candle to help us see better."

"*Grazie.* Now, I have three letters, but you can just read them in whatever order you want. I think this one is from my sister," the woman said, picking up an envelope. "It looks like her writing."

"Okay, let's see what we have here." Rosa shuffled through the envelopes and picked one up and opened it. She unfolded it and began to read, the friend watching her every move and listening intently to every word. A tissue dabbed an eye every now and then and more than once a smile curled the friend's lips.

Rosa had somehow or another found herself being approached by several of the illiterate Italians, and was soon reading letters and writing dictated replies for her fellow countrymen. Letters from their own friends and family were very precious and treasured, and Rosa was more than willing to lend a hand to the less fortunate.

"Giovanna," Rosa said, glancing up, "would you, please, get me some paper."

Giovanna sighed, but got up.

"*Grazie,*" said Rosa. She laid the paper out flat and began to write.

That night at dinner, conversation dwelt on the events of the day.

"I see that the Maffia's been around," said Raffaele. "I'm so glad you were all safely inside when it happened."

"Ah, what can we do to keep them away?" Rosa pitied. "Just terrible, very terrible . . ."

"What did they do, Papa? Mama wouldn't let us go outside all afternoon," said Grazia.

Raffaele smiled at his wife. "That was very wise of her." Turning back to Grazia, he answered, "They bombed the store out front, messed it up pretty bad, too."

"Where any of the front apartments damaged?" asked Rosa as she served her husband a second serving.

"I couldn't tell. I'm just glad that ours is at the back of the building..."

* * *

"Now, be sure to pick the best vegetables, just the way I've shown you," instructed Rosa. "Check the flour too, see that it's nice and fresh—the way I like it."

"But isn't Papa bringing home the vegetables and fruit?" asked Grazia. "The fruit and vegetables he gets from working at the market are always so delicious."

"Yes, but I'll be needing more than the usual amount for the christening dinner we'll be having. This baby is coming soon and I want to be all ready," said Rosa. She rattled on as Grazia nodded her comprehension, anxious to leave. Antonio squirmed in his sister's arms as the younger girls chattered impatiently by the door.

"You girls cooperate for Grazia, and don't wander off. Don't talk to strangers, you hear? And be sure you are home before dark. Oh, and Donatine, fill the pitcher while you're out, please. We're nearly out of wine and we'll be needing more for dinner." Finally, Rosa shooed them out into the winter air. It was the dead of winter, their second in America, and Rosa watched out the window as a light snow began to fall. Starting with the very first errand she'd run in America, Rosa always took her daughters along with her to do the shopping. Today was different, however. The baby was due any day now, and Rosa was too tired to walk the streets for food.

They'll be fine, Rosa comforted herself. She lay back under a thick blanket and closed her eyes. *They've watched me shop dozens of times.*

The girls *had* watched her dozens of times, knowing well that her hands were guided by years of experience. Rosa would instruct as she went along, teaching her daughters the art of keeping house. With one touch, her gentle hands determined the usefulness of produce, freshness of flour and spice. Her chubby figure would knowingly dart towards the next item on her list, as she completed the errands systematically. Rosa was simply a lady, and though there were, at times, more than a few pairs of ears that would have rather turned in another direction, her daughters loved and adored her.

Down in the streets, the girls busied themselves with gathering the items on the list.

"Let's hurry so that we can be back to the tenement before Mr. Burnstein gets there," said Maria.

"Yeah. It would be quicker if we split up, though, don't you think?" Michaelina suggested. "Mama would never find out anyhow."

"She would if some of us got lost," said Grazia in her observant way. "We'd better stay together. It shouldn't take us too much longer. Come on everybody." She led the way from grocery cart to grocery cart until they were finally heading to the local church building where Donatine bought wine to fill the pitcher from home.

"There," said Donatine when she finished. "Let's go!"

They reached Twenty-sixth Second Avenue just in time. Mr. Burnstein was just blowing his whistle as the girls appeared around the corner. Ahead of them, they could see other children running through the crowds.

"There's Mr. Burnstein, there's Mr. Burnstein!" the girls yelled to one another as they ran toward the tenement. Mr. Burnstein owned the apartment houses and came once a month to collect the rents. A sturdy man, Mr. Burnstein, dressed in spats and a derby, was walking slowly with his cane.

"Stand back my lads and lasses, stand back . . ." cried Mr. Burnstein above the noise in the street.

The Marone girls slid to a halt just a few feet from Mr. Burnstein and caught their breath while the rest of the local immigrant children gathered behind and around them. Everyone waited, with Mr. Burnstein exhibiting the most patience, for the little crippled boy to come forward. He lived not too far from the Marones' apartment, and always had to be the first to greet Mr. Burnstein.

"There, there," smiled Mr. Burnstein when the young lad had reached him. "How's my little chap this fine wintery day?"

"Just fine, sir. And how about yourself?"

"Well, I'm doing okay, but I think that I woke up two pennies too rich this morning. How about you take these and go buy yourself a treat, huh?" Mr. Burnstein's smile broadened as the youngster held out a bony hand, shaking slightly from the coldness of the air.

"Fine, sir. Thank you!"

The remaining forty-plus children knew what was coming next. Even so, Mr. Burnstein pretended to be worried about his pocketbook.

"Don't you think you youngins could help me out? Here, two pennies each for a treat. Go on, and enjoy the day!"

"Thank you, Mr. Burnstein."

"Goodbye, Mister."

"Thanks!"

The Marones' children ran to the nearest candy store to spend their pennies, then sauntered back through the streets toward home.

* * *

"Another girl," announced the doctor, laying the newborn Marone in Rosa's arms. "And a beautiful one at that." It was January 9, 1913, and Rocchitella Rita Marone had just been born. She was welcomed, like her brother, into the world by the busyness of city life. Immigrant life. A life that, while surrounded by love and family, was not without pain and heartache; no more than life in Laurenzana had been. Rocchitella, Ella for short, soon became ill.

"We must hurry and get her baptized," said Rosa, her deeply rooted Catholic faith shining forth once again. Turning to Grazia, she added with a smile, "That food you bought the other day was neither too early nor too late."

"I'll tend to the preparations, Mama," Grazia offered. "You lie in bed and rest; you just had a baby."

The girls worked long hours at the table, mixing, rolling, cutting, folding, filling, cooking, baking, stirring, testing and cooling. Finally, meticulously made pasta, with all the trimmings and side dishes, was completed and set aside for the following day's celebration.

"You girls have done a wonderful job," approved Rosa as the girls' success lay on a large board on the table. "Tomorrow's celebration will be perfect, thanks to your hard work and long hours at the table. Here, one of you, help me carry this board over here," motioned Rosa. She picked up one end of the board and waited for assistance.

"But where are you going to put it, Mama?"

"Under the bed, where it can be out of the way."

The girls giggled, but complied with her wish. Before long, they were in bed and getting their rest for the big day that was ahead. But early the next morning, when the pasta was rescued for boiling, Rosa discovered an awful detail involved with tenement life.

"But where did it go?" the girls asked in dismay. "Don't tell me Papa ate it . . ."

Rosa chuckled. "No, your *padre* didn't eat it. Mice did."

Within a few short months, Antonio had welcomed Ella into his little world. She had gotten well quickly and Antonio, almost two, was anxious for a playmate.

"Ella, come play, come play!"

"Antonio," Rosa would laugh, "Ella's too tiny to play."

But Antonio would persist, and persist himself to tears unless one of his older sisters came to his rescue in time.

"Here, Antonio, come play with me," Donatine might suggest, and for hours Antonio would be kept happy.

Then one day, fate hit. Antonio suddenly became deathly ill, and several weeks passed without a single sign of recovery. Deep-chest coughs shook his small frame and doctors sadly lowered their heads. "He has bronchitis," one diagnosed and soon after, pneumonia was suspected.

"There's nothing that can be done. I'm terribly sorry."

On May 7, 1913, Antonio died. There was no opportunity to question a mass grave, and the Marones wept as they said goodbye to their second son.

* * *

"Okay, then we'll go," said Raffaele. "It will be no problem to have a family picture taken, if that's what you want." It had been five months since Antonio had died, and Raffaele assured his wife that he would check in on a photographer. He stood to go. "I will see what I can find out before I come home tonight. *Addio, Rosa, chi bella Rosa!*" It wasn't very long before an appointment with a photographer had been negotiated. Standing in front of them with his camera on his tripod and blanket in hand, he waited for the Marones to be ready.

"Grazia, your collar is crooked. Maria, help Donatine straighten her stockings. Oh Michaelina, come over here and let me fix your hair bow." Rosa was in a scurry.

"All right!" cried Raffaele with dwindling patience. "Everyone just get in their places and look at the camera."

Faces snapped to stern attention, hands rested on a nearby shoulder. Crisp white dresses contrasted with dark stockings and shoes. Little Ella made a momentary squirm, but Raffaele's grip on her belly managed to keep her still while the first camera flash that the Marones had ever experienced filled the room.

CHAPTER TWENTY-TWO

The Guest from Hartford

With the end of summer came a brilliantly colored fall, or at least it would have been colorful if the big city buildings did not crowd out the countryside trees. The wind did its best to bring the leaves to the city, though, and piles of them collected in the gutters, street corners and alleyways. Small whirlwinds carried some of the leaves out into the middle of the street where they were trampled and brushed aside by the passers-by.

Fall meant back to school for the girls. While Grazia was sixteen and no longer attending, Michaelina proudly took her place among Giovanna and Maria.

"*Addio*, Mama! *Addio*, Grazia! *Addio* Ella!" Off to school they would trot, learning new things and bringing home lots of homework to show for it. Each day seemed to bring a new friend into their acquaintance, and they were only waiting for their *madre's* listening ear, which was always interested in their day's activities. Coming home was perhaps the best part of school for Michaelina. Delicious aromas met her nose the minute the door was opened, and all the day's troubles would be lost as everyone sat down for another evening at home.

One afternoon, the girls returned to the apartment to find a guest seated at the table.

"Good afternoon, girls," said Rosa when they opened the door and stepped inside.

"Good afternoon, Mama," came their reply. They systematically stepped out of their galoshes and took off their sweaters, while they each munched on a slice of watermelon.

"Ah, you've been to your godmother's I see," Rosa smiled. "I trust she is doing well?"

"Yes," said Michaelina as she and the others approached the table with their books. "And she gave me an *extra* penny today, because I'm going to school now. So I bought some watermelon with one of the pennies, and am going to buy some candy with the other penny." As Michaelina took another bite of the juicy fruit, Maria cut in.

"Well, I still have more than you because I lit some stoves the other day, and plus when Mr. Burnstein comes next week that'll be even more . . ."

"Lit some stoves?" asked Donatine.

"Yes, the Jews around here don't believe in working on Saturdays. If you're walking past them, and they happen to need their stoves lit, they'll pay you to go inside and do it for them . . ."

"Oh," said Donatine. "Who's Mr. Burnstein?"

"And Mama," Michaelina chattered just as Maria was about to answer Donatine. She sat down and opened her books. "Today at school the teacher said my new name is Margaret, but Mama, I don't have to have it if I don't want to, right Mama?"

Rosa raised her hand to quiet them. "Girls, you can work on your homework later, or somewhere else now." She glanced at the guest, and then back at her daughters. Their eyes returned her gaze with skepticism. Often when they arrived home from school, there were friends or neighbors seated at the table for tea or conversation, but rarely was it someone so important that homework could not be tackled in their presence.

"Hmm," shrugged Michaelina indifferently. She glanced at Donatine, and they both got up to leave the room. What they didn't notice, however, was the look the visitor was giving Grazia. Or rather, the look that was passing between them both. It was the first time they had set eyes on one another, yet a common factor seemed to pass between them.

"Ah, here's Raffaele," said Rosa later that evening. When Raffaele entered and began to take off his hat and coat, Rosa turned in her chair. "Look who's come for a visit." She gestured towards the table, where the guest still sat. The children were within ear shot and whispering filled their corner of the room.

Raffaele, more or less moved by the visitor, wiped his shoes. "*Buona sera*, Rocco Rizzo," he said finally. "Did you have a good trip?" Raffaele crossed the room and pulled out a chair at the table.

"Girls, come help prepare dinner," Rosa called as she left the table. Turning to Donatine she said, "Run along to the tavern and get some wine for dinner, please."

"Yes, Mama," said Donatine as she took the pitcher from Rosa and hastened toward the door. She grabbed the necessary coins and slipped out into the hall. Her footsteps could be heard from inside the apartment as she clattered down the hall and stairways.

The other girls turned their attention back to the guest, whom they were beginning to recognize. "Yes, I arrived here without incident," he was saying. "The weather in Hartford was most pleasant when I left, but I didn't think twice about leaving it. No, not for the reason I've come." The guest shook his head and smiled. His mouth opened as if to say more, but Raffaele interrupted.

"No, I don't imagine so. But, I think it would be best to talk about all of that later this evening."

The girls' shoulders slumped at their father's wish, and their minds began to race. Dinner was served and devoured by nine hungry persons and Raffaele succeeded in limiting the conversation to small talk. The girls' day at school, Rosa's activities at home and Raffaele's day at work never seemed more boring and unimportant. Time had never seemed to pass so quickly, nor the day ever seemed so short when Raffaele sent the girls off to bed.

With dinner finished and the children in bed, Rosa and Raffaele sat at an empty table with their guest, sipping cups of hot coffee.

"I understand that you have been waiting for a long time to marry her, but Grazia is simply too young," said Raffaele. His features had never been more stern and decided. Visions of his conversation that had taken place with Donato Pavese years before rushed through his mind. He could almost hear his own voice pleading for permission to marry the love of his life.

"But Mr. Marone, I would be good to her. I'm settled and I've got a job; I could support a wife and family with no problem." Rocco Rizzo was determined and his voice rose as he spoke. "I love her. I ask your permission, please!"

"No. I said no, and I mean no. Rosa and I have discussed this, Rocco, and we have decided that Grazia is too young right now to get married." Their voices carried into the adjacent rooms, where the girls were sleeping. Rather, where they were lying in their beds, listening. Grazia was especially attentive, though she might not have readily admitted it, and the other girls were whispering among themselves. They could hear someone pacing the room, and from the tone of the voices, it could have easily been either of the two men. Rosa was no doubt sitting quietly at the table.

"When Grazia was born," Giovanna explained in a low voice, "Mama and Papa, and Rocco Rizzo's parents, paired the two children together. They decided that when both children grew up, they'd get married." She went on to explain that when Rocco had grown older, he had come to America, where he lived in a town called Hartford.

"Will Grazia go away to Hartford?" whispered Donatine with concern.

"No, not right now anyway. Papa seems pretty determined about not letting Grazia and Rocco get married." Giovanna turned onto her stomach under the covers. "I heard Mama once say that she was sixteen when she got married . . ."

The conversation between the two men resumed and the girls listened carefully. "Just let me try, Mr. Marone. We'd only be in Hartford, if you weren't satisfied."

"No," said Raffaele flatly, glancing at his wife. Turning back to Rocco Rizzo, he said, "I will not allow you to marry her at this time." He paused, holding his guest's gaze. "But, let's say that in three more years both of you are still single, and you want to come back and ask me again, I will be more inclined to give you my permission then."

The next day on the way to school, the girls' conversation

from the night before continued. "I'm glad that Papa said no," stated Michaelina, "I don't want Grazia to leave yet."

Giovanna looked down at her sister. "Don't worry, Rocco Rizzo shouldn't be coming back for another few years. You'll have plenty of time to enjoy Grazia before she leaves home."

"Who is Rocco Rizzo anyway?" asked Michaelina. She stopped walking to pick up a bright leaf. "He's not related to us, is he?"

"Not yet," laughed Maria. The other girls giggled, but quieted so Giovanna could reply.

"His family lived near us in Laurenzana. You probably don't remember, but we went to their house many times and we walked past it often. They're property owners, just like mother and father, and I'd even guess that they still live in the same house."

"Most people do," said Maria as they neared the school. She noticed a friend several yards away and waved. "Unless, of course, they move to America."

CHAPTER TWENTY-THREE

Help Wanted

The cool weather changed to winter snows and brought with it, no doubt, thoughts of home. The Christmas treats and holiday visitors added their seasonal cheer, but deep inside, perhaps when all were under warm covers at night, Rosa longed for Laurenzana. Feeling homesick was common among the women that Rosa visited. For most of them, their husbands had promised that the passing of time would bring a better life and easier times. For Rosa, however, there was a different promise that she was clinging to. And the coming of 1914 reminded her of it.

I can take her back to America with me and we'll stay for say, six years. After the six years, we'll come back here and discuss it further.

The Christmas cheer brought with it a momentary distraction for Rosa, when she discovered that their eighth child was on the way. If Raffaele thought five girls and a toddling Antonio had been rowdy and noisome, his opinion had certainly remained unchanged. Another baby meant more noise and chaos, more people and toys to trip over and . . . less of Raffaele.

"Michaelina, Donatine," Rosa called.

"Yes, Mama?"

"Go and find your *padre*. Dinner is ready and almost on the table. Run along, quick, quick."

"Yes, Mama."

The girls threw on their winter garments and dashed out the apartment door and through the tenement halls. The winter weather did not seem to have slowed anyone down and the girls found the streets as busy and crowded as usual.

"Let's go to the movie house first today," Michaelina yelled as she pulled her sister in and out among the men, women and children. "That's where he was yesterday."

"Okay," said Donatine. She scooted quickly to the side to dart a parked cart. "And I hope he's there because I'm so starved and Mama's meal smelled so good I just can't wait any longer for dinner."

The girls ran until they reached the side street for the movie house. They entered through the big door quite out of breath and looked around.

"Oh no," Michaelina groaned. "He's not here."

"Well," said Donatine, looking on the bright side. "That only means one thing. If Papa's not at the movie house, he's at the club house . . ."

Back outdoors, back through the crowded streets, up Second Avenue, through the door, into the midst of the small Democratic Party gathering.

"Well, if it isn't my own little daughters," said Raffaele as he turned to the men around him.

"Papa, dinner's ready."

"You can come home now, Papa. Mama's waiting."

"Don't you have a cheery little family, Rockefeller? What a nice little chirp . . ." A hand or two reached out to pat the girls' heads or gently pinch their cheeks as their mittened hands led Raffaele out of the club house toward home.

Though it might not have been evident at the time, Ella's first birthday was a prelude to a year of changes for the Marones. With a growing family who lived the lifestyle they lived, Raffaele was having difficulty keeping up.

"I'm just not earning enough money," he confessed to his wife one evening. "This whole thing is not working out the way we planned." He raised his arms as if suggesting his surrender.

Rosa sipped her coffee as she contemplated her reply. "Well," she said finally. "How did you used to keep up?"

"It was very different when I was here alone." Raffaele leaned forward and rested his arms on the table. "First of all, it didn't take much to keep myself clothed, fed and housed. Secondly . . ."

"No," interrupted Rosa, "I mean when we first came here. We've been in America with you for almost three years, dear, and just now things have begun to change."

Raffaele sighed and sat back. "A lot has changed. For one thing, I am now paying to keep four children enrolled in school, I have the apartment rent to pay, more mouths and bigger stomachs to fill . . ."

"And another one on the way," smiled Rosa as she patted her belly.

Raffaele continued, not tickled. "More mouths to fill, a toddler who is desperate to explore the world and, as if that's not enough," he added with another sigh, "your health is all but superb."

"Oh don't you worry about me," said Rosa. She waved her hand through the air. "I'm fine."

"No, you're not fine. Every night I come home from work and find your head or back aching, your nose running or something else is ailing you. It's just not working out."

"Well, what do you suggest that we do?"

"I don't really know. I do know, however, that jobs as a shoe polisher, bartender and fruit stand proprietor are just not bringing in the necessary amount of money." Raffaele sat back in his chair to contemplate. Rosa, on the other hand, was full of thoughts.

"*Madre* and *padre* would certainly be surprised if we arrived back in Laurenzana three years early."

"I do not plan to fall back on them," stated Raffaele, suddenly sitting more upright. "The life you lived back there was an entirely different matter, Rosa. We are in America now, where what you see and work for is what you get. America is all about cutting your own path, and building your own life." He paused to make sure Rosa was listening. "America is not about living a life run by hired hands; that was Laurenzana. That was when you had acres and acres to raise your own crops. See, you didn't need lots of money back there, Rosa. You were living off the land."

"Okay, so . . . what do you suggest?" The repeated question drove Raffaele to silence. "Well, if you don't have a suggestion, then I do. Why don't we send one of the children to work? They can work hard, just like anyone else, and that would solve the momentary financial problem. They would also meet new people, and it would be good experience all the way around."

Raffaele stared, but then smiled. "All right, you've solved our problem. The next step is to decide which child to send to work. But," Raffaele scooted out his chair and rose, "since your genius mind came up with the idea, I'll let you come up with the child of your choice. *Buona notte.*"

A few nights later, during a delicious Italian-style meal, Rosa broke the news. "Your *padre* and I have decided that we need a second income for our family." The girls swapped glances and gazed at their parents.

"But, why?" one of the girls asked.

"Well," said Rosa, "each of you is growing older, and needs different things, like a good education; that costs money. And then there are still more babies coming," Rosa patted her small belly, "and that means another mouth to fill. Then, of course, everyone needs new clothes and shoes, and . . ."

A whoop from the girls created an interruption. "Okay, so who's the lucky one?"

Rosa smiled and paused a few moments, watching the tension grow. "I have decided on Giovanna. I've lined up a job for you, and you'll be starting the day after tomorrow." Rosa glanced at Giovanna. "We'll be counting on you to work hard; your *padre* is determined to overcome this struggle with your help."

CHAPTER TWENTY-FOUR

Rosa's Not Well

The money earned by Raffaele and Giovanna's individual jobs proved momentarily sufficient for the expenses at hand. By the time September arrived, bringing with it the new Marone baby, several necessary items in the apartment had been replaced and few worn clothes and shoes remained. Nook and cranny alike had been swept or scrubbed clean and fresh air blew through the apartment windows. The world that Rosa and the girls had worked hard to create for the new baby proved warm and welcoming. Anna Rosa Marone arrived on September 14, 1914.

With Giovanna out of school, there were only two girls to keep enrolled, and Anna didn't demand too much right away. Fall passed and winter approached, bringing with it, of course, another Christmas and holiday season.

"Mama, baby want cookie. Baby want cookie." An almost three year old Ella climbed up onto a chair while Rosa worked at the table.

"Does baby want cookie, or does Ella want cookie?" laughed Grazia, looking on. She and Donatine were helping with the baking.

"No, no, no. Baby can't have cookie, and neither can you," laughed Rosa. "You go play with your toys, Ella. You can have one of these after your dinner." Rosa shooed away the toddler and continued her work. She rolled, cut, shaped and twisted, her hands forming the dough in just the right way. Her touch of expertise created a temptation to fingers to creep onto the table in hope of snitching a bit of sweet, anis-filled piece of dough. But Rosa's quick eyes caught every move every time, and her flour-coated hand would creep across the table and slap away any culprit.

Whether they liked it or not, Maria and Michaelina joined the culinary work when they arrived from school. Christmas preparations held priority over homework. "Put your books down and come to help," said Rosa many an afternoon. "We still have two more batches of these to make, and the ones baking are just about ready to be taken out to cool. C'mon, get your aprons on."

"Mama, but we have lots of homework," the girls complained.

"Mmm-hmm, and you have all evening to finish it." A knowing smile soon crept onto Rosa's face. "Today was your last day until after Christmas, so you have an entire month to finish that homework." Her motherly way of being direct and gentle all at the same time won out every time, and Rosa proved her ability to manage her seven children well amid minimized household space and a small pool of finances.

Grazia turned eighteen in March, 1915, and her quickened growth towards adulthood, in addition to the occasional visits from Rocco Rizzo, caused Rosa to worry. The possibility of her daughter's marriage left Rosa wondering how she would ever manage back in Italy. *I'd miss her so much, more so than I do my own madre.* But there was no denying reality.

"*Ciao, ciao.*"

"Oh Rocco. Come in, come in," said Rosa as she tended a batch of pastries at the table. "Grazia, take his coat and Maria, get him some coffee, please." Rosa's flour-coated hands waved through the air as she welcomed Rocco Rizzo into the already crowded room. The warmth, the congeniality, the love, the family and the laughter was enough to beckon anyone in from out of the cold.

"Ah, a hot drink on a day like today is the absolute best thing in the world," said Rocco, sitting down in the midst of the household livelihood. Conversation about Hartford, life in New York, school, Raffaele's work and daily activities helped the winter days slip by more pleasantly.

"Grazia," smiled Rocco one evening. The whole family was once again gathered at the table and a hearty portion of the meal filled each plate. "It's a gorgeous evening out there. What'd you say we go to the opera together?"

Grazia's eyes sparkled. "The opera? It sounds wonderful."

"Eh, eh, eh," interjected Raffaele. "Not unless you take all of the girls, Rocco."

Rocco's smile disappeared, and Grazia's eyes lost their sparkle. Rocco looked around at all the girls he'd have to escort through the darkness, all of the girls he'd have to keep an eye on at the opera, all of the girls he'd have to spend the evening with.

"Forget it, Grazia . . ."

The onset of summer found the Marones expecting another baby. However, the pregnancy, in addition to the enjoyable family life, did not hide from Raffaele the underlying stress that Rosa was experiencing.

"*Rosa, chi bella Rosa.*" Raffaele smiled down at his wife shortly after the children had retired one evening. "You aren't doing well. You're over tired, and just look at you, three different nights this week I've come home to the girls running errands, or tending dinner and the babies while you rest."

But Rosa would have none of it. "I'm fine," she insisted. "It's early now, and I'm sure the extra sleep will be the one remedy I need."

"But, you've said that before," he reminded. "Back before Giovanna began working your health was poor. And you still aren't doing much better."

"Really, Raffaele. I'm sure the pregnancy is just making me more tired, and with Ella, my, what a fireball, she keeps me running. I've just had a lot going lately. I'll be fine, dear." She smiled as she slid from his grasp. "*Buona notte.*"

But Raffaele wasn't satisfied. He allowed a few more months to pass before he confronted her again. This time he did more than ask a question or make a suggestion.

CHAPTER TWENTY-FIVE

Good News ... Bad News

"Rosa, I've scheduled a doctor's appointment for you," said Raffaele one morning in late fall. He stood by the apartment door with hat in hand. "He agreed that you should not be feeling so bad on such a regular basis. Perhaps his diagnosis will reveal something that we can work toward eliminating."

"All right, dear," sighed Rosa.

A few days later, Rosa bustled around the apartment. "Now, I want you to do the errands that I told you, and I don't want you to get into trouble," she told the girls as she picked up a stray toy. "Be sure to stay together, and don't put Ella down. Oh," she added with stressed concern, "and don't come home too late. Or too early."

The girls stood impatiently at the door as she rattled on. The moment Rosa was through, the girls dashed out the door. The girls spent the afternoon in freedom, somehow managing to stay out of trouble.

They arrived home well after the doctor had left. "What did he say, Mama?"

"Oh, he said I'm fine," smiled Rosa, waving her hand through the air. Changing the subject, she asked the girls to help with dinner as she stood stirring a pot of thick and creamy sauce, flavored with chunks of tomatoes. At dinner the question was repeated, and with Raffaele present, Rosa couldn't get away with another vague answer.

"He said that it's certainly nothing serious," said Rosa, buttering a warm slice of bread.

"Well, that's good," said Raffaele. "Did he pinpoint the problem, though?"

Rosa fumbled. "Well, he said some fresher air might help. But, that's ridiculous, besides, we'll be going back to Laurenzana soon, and I'm sure everything will clear up then. Come now," she said as she glanced around the table, "everyone eat up."

It was several more months before Raffaele had the opportunity to confront Rosa again. Donatine had become enrolled in school when the fall term began, and the preparations had kept Rosa preoccupied. In addition, the list of things to be completed before the new baby arrived only tired Rosa further, and there weren't many evenings that she stayed up much later than the children. When Raffaele's opportunity did arrive, it was just before the Christmas bustle.

"So, tell me again what the doctor said when he came," said Raffaele. He set down his daily paper and turned to his wife.

Rosa sighed, setting her mending project in her lap. "It's nothing really, Raffaele. Your worries are just causing the children undue anxiety. Please, just let it be."

Raffaele shook his head, though Rosa was too busy concentrating on her stitches to notice. "No, I want to know what he said."

Rosa sighed again. "He asked me a lot of questions, like how I felt and when I felt better or worse. I explained everything to him. Before he left, he said that the city air probably had a lot to do with the way I've been feeling." Rosa paused and put up a finger. "I didn't feel like this back in Laurenzana. And I didn't start feeling like this until we'd been here for sometime. Anyhow," she concluded as she returned to her sewing, "he said that getting back into some fresher air would most likely solve my problem." A smile filled her face as she noted, "We're coming up on the five-year mark, Raffaele. I'd be more than willing to hold out for another year; when we get back to Laurenzana, everything will be fine."

Raffaele did not share her positivity. Perceiving so, Rosa added, "Raffaele, it's not all bad. Besides, this place would be a happier one if we all stopped worrying about my health. I think we could make this next year very enjoyable, if we all try hard enough. Come on, let's try."

"It's not that," said Raffaele. He shook his head.

"Well, what is it then?" Rosa could tell something was bothering her husband, and she leaned from her chair to rest a hand on Raffaele's arm. "Raffaele?"

"I, well . . . it's just that . . ." Raffaele stalled for his words. "Well, I know this is hard for you to understand, Rosa, but . . . we're not going back to Laurenzana."

CHAPTER TWENTY-SIX

Life Without Grazia

Christmas came and went, and with it a bitter-sweet celebration. Rosa did her best to keep her spirits up, but the thought of remaining in America was heartbreaking. Though it had been several weeks since Raffaele had confronted her, Rosa did not have it in her to write the letter to her parents. Not yet anyway.

"We had everything back in Laurenzana," she recalled complaining to Raffaele. "A big house, lots of land, property, livestock, hired help. Now look at us, we can hardly keep standing."

"I know, Rosa, but it's just better this way." Raffaele's words played over and over in Rosa's mind. "The fact that we had so much, and were so well off back in Italy, is the precise point of the matter. We left all of that to start a new life here; we can't just uproot and abandon the progress we've worked so hard to make. Please, Rosa," his pleadings filled her every thought, "you must try to understand. Stopping now would only preface a more difficult time back in Italy. We have to keep going."

"But, but . . ." Rosa and the girls had lived their new life with fervor, knowing that each passing day, regardless of its struggles and difficulties, was bringing them closer to their home back in Italy. Now the light at the end of the tunnel had disappeared. The months passed. Though no one seemed especially attentive to the occasions, Raffaele and Rosa added another year to their wedding anniversary, Ella turned three, Maria turned fourteen and Grazia turned nineteen.

Shortly after Grazia's birthday, the new baby arrived. Antonetta Marie Marone was born on March 14, 1916 and came at a time when the Marones were focusing hard on other things. Rocco Rizzo had made his appearance again and everyone knew what that meant.

"It's been three years, Mr. Marone," said Rocco Rizzo.

"Mmm-hmm," nodded Raffaele, picking up a freshly baked pastry. He took a bite before he replied. "And is that all you've come to New York to do? Tell me that it's been three years since we visited last?" A smile crept onto his face, revealing a momentary lull in his stern personality.

"No," said Rocco Rizzo hurriedly. "I, uh . . . well in case you've forgotten, I've come back to ask you, once again, for permission to marry Grazia." He sat on the edge of his seat, anxious for the coming reply. Raffaele cleared his throat, and looked over at Rosa. She was engaged in a mending project, and paused to return his glance.

"Yes, Rocco, you may marry her."

After weeks of planning, baking, sewing and preparing, the wedding was celebrated. On April 30, 1916, Rosa held a month-and-a-half old bundle of Antonetta in her arms as her oldest daughter walked down the isle. The newly wedded couple was congratulated and wished farewell as they left for their home in Hartford. They planned to settle on the second floor of the three-level apartment house that Rocco owned.

Over the next couple of months, the absence of Grazia was quickly noticed around the apartment. With Giovanna at work and Maria, Michaelina and Donatine at school all day, Rosa's days were full. She had a house to run, and two toddling children who managed to remain underfoot all day long. In addition, Rosa's health was not improving.

"Ella, take Anna over there to play with the toys. Mother's trying to make dinner and I can't have her underfoot." Just as Ella and Anna managed to get out of Rosa's way, Antonetta would scream or demand attention in another way. When the girls returned from school, homework would be set aside so that dinner could be completed, or the baby rocked, or the toddlers quieted. The arrival of summer cheered Rosa up a bit, since the girls would be able to help her during the day.

"Here, run these errands for me, please," Rosa would say, anxious to resume her household duties without interruption. "And take special care to keep Ella from running off. The last thing I need is a lost child." If there were no errands to run or no food to be bought, shooing the girls behind a closed door worked as well for Rosa. "Just take these toys in there and close the door behind you, and mind you, keep them distracted until I'm finished mopping the floor."

Keeping the young ones out of Rosa's way, and out from under her feet was, perhaps, one of the highest priorities on her list. Once successful, Rosa didn't worry about her babies, confident as she was in her older daughters' abilities to tend them properly.

"Michaelina, listen to this," laughed Maria as she held up a magazine. She relaxed on the bed and began to read the article aloud, while Michaelina, reclining on the daybed, became deeply engaged. Around them Ella and Anna played with toys on what little floor space remained, the nearby door closed in confining authority. Magazine pages continued to turn as Maria read for several minutes, and Michaelina scooted up close to peer over her sister's shoulder.

"*Addio*, Maria. *Addio* . . ." waved Ella, but her sisters weren't listening. The magazine hiding their faces, and the contents tightly holding their attention, Maria and Michaelina took no notice as Ella and Anna slipped out of the room. Several more minutes passed before the article was finished, and when the girls were through discussing it, they groaned.

"Aw, we better go get Ella and Anna. They no doubt went straight to mother, looking for a cookie or something." The girls got up and dashed out of the room, knowing that Rosa would be disappointed in them. When they opened the door, smoke stung their eyes.

"Oh no, fire!" Maria and Michaelina suddenly hit the floor, crawling on all fours. "Mama!" they called, crawling towards the center of the main room where there appeared to be an area free of smoke.

"Quiet down, girls, I'm right here," called Rosa from behind the door of the third room, where she was putting Antonetta down for a nap. It was a crowded room, with a bed, dresser and crib and Rosa took her time in exiting the room. When she finally came tiptoeing through the door, she screamed.

"Fire! Fire!" She dashed at once back into the bedroom and grabbed her sleeping baby. Maria and Michaelina had reached the center of the room, and could hear whimpering sounds. The girls parted, and Maria called out, "Ella, Anna!" She dove in the direction of the noise and groped for her sisters. Though her eyes were almost squeezed shut, she could see two small figures sitting beside each other in the midst of the smoke. Filling each fist with a handful of clothing, Maria pulled the toddlers into the center of the room. At the same time, Rosa entered with Antonetta.

"Bring her to the center of the room, Mama, the smoke is thinner there. I'll go fetch water."

Maria rose and as she dashed for the door, she noticed the pail of the morning's dish water. She sighed with relief and ran to pick it up. The water in the bucket splashed over the sides as she scurried across the room. Ella and Anna sat, rubbing their eyes and crying. Mother handed Antonette to Michaelina and turned to comfort her young daughters.

"Come on dears, come sit down with me." Rosa beckoned her daughters to the other side of the room. "The smoke is even thinner over here. Come on, sit with me."

Ella and Anna followed Rosa to the day bed and cuddled up. Their whimpers slackened as they watched Maria bring the water to the fire. The smoke grew thicker and slightly black as she dumped the water. The flames soon sizzled into oblivion and Maria stepped back, coughing and waving her hand through the air to clear the smoke. As she did so, she laughed aloud.

"What's so funny?" asked Rosa, crossing the room to get a closer look. Michaelina followed.

"Look at that," pointed Maria. She began to laugh once more as she looked down into the box. "Diapers. A charred box of burnt diapers."

Maybe Rosa laughed, maybe she cried. Maybe she scolded Maria and Michaelina for not tending to their responsibilities. Whatever the case, Ella turned to Anna, and smiled that determined little grin.

CHAPTER TWENTY-SEVEN

Goodbye, New York

Summer passed much too quickly, and as the girls returned to school, Rosa once again struggled to maintain her well being. Giovanna worked hard to supply a decent second income, and the family benefited from her efforts. Maria was no longer enrolled in school, and had joined her sister and *padre* at work. Rosa was used to Maria's absence from the apartment, and whether she was at school or at work did not make much difference. Except, of course, that one was drawing money out of the canning jar and one was putting money into it.

The passing of time brought with it a constant need of repairs on the clothing and household items. This kept Rosa and the girls, when they had the time, busy with ongoing sewing, knitting, mending and darning projects.

"*Rosa, chi bella Rosa*, you're health is still not good," said Raffaele once again. He knew that the upcoming date of their planned return to Laurenzana played a large part in his wife's distress, and he treaded carefully when speaking to her.

"And what do you suggest?" said Rosa. She jabbed her needle into the material with force as she spoke, holding back a great sea of emotions. She pursed her lips together as she waited for his reply.

"Well, I thought that since you miss Grazia an awful lot," said Raffaele slowly, "and since moving out of the city would help your health, that we could move to Connecticut." He sat forward in the chair, resting his elbows on his knees. He slowly rubbed his hands together as he spoke. "It would be up to you, of course. But the idea would certainly meet your needs, and solve most of your problems."

Rosa sewed busily, seeming as if she had not heard her husband's suggestion. Finally she replied. "I would definitely like to see Grazia, and live closer to her. And it would be nice to feel better again." Rosa set her sewing on her lap and sighed. "And I certainly wouldn't mind leaving this place."

"Okay." Raffaele clapped a hand on each knee as he rose. "What do you say I go ahead and see what Connecticut has to offer? You can stay back and pack us up."

It was several months later before Raffaele returned with news of a place to live.

"Where is it, Papa?" the girls asked anxiously.

"Is it near Grazia's house?"

"Is it big?"

"All right, all right, one question at a time. The house is on Park Street in Hartford and yes, it's near Grazia's house. It's not gigantic, but it's bigger than this place."

At the thought of larger living quarters, the girls began their own conversations about what it might be like. Rosa closed the last box and approached Raffaele about a job for himself.

"Yes, I found one at the Underwood Typewriter Company."

"That's wonderful," said Rosa with a smile. "How far will you need to travel?"

"Not far. It's close enough for me to walk to," said Raffaele. He glanced beyond his wife. The girls were laughing and making a racket in the empty house.

"*Grande**!" said Ella, raising her arms and running around the empty rooms. Anna followed her.

"Well, until all of us move in," laughed Donatine. She and Michaelina stood at the window. "Remember when we first moved in, it looked gigantic. Then all our stuff crowded the rooms."

"Yeah, and you were scared to live near a jailhouse," laughed Michaelina, nudging Donatine.

"I was not," defended Donatine. "You stop it, Michaelina, that's not nice."

Raffaele called them to order and motioned towards the center of the room. "Let's get going. Everybody grab something and help carry this stuff out." Rosa and the girls had worked hard, and with the belongings of seven girls and two adults, a healthy pile of bundles and boxes lay before them.

As suddenly as they'd come, Raffaele and his family left the tenement. Left the busy streets. Left New York. Thoughts of the first days and weeks in New York were contemplated as the busyness of city life grew quieter and smaller behind them. Old friends, who had been there to help them overcome the fears and struggles upon their arrival, were faithfully among the crowds, waving farewell and hollering wishes of luck and good fortune.

The fresher air began to have its effect on Rosa, and the entire family benefited from her change in demeanor. She was once again that gentle, chubby figure who could whip up a five-course meal, complete with several batches of pastries, while keeping Ella and Anna out of trouble and an eye on Antonetta.

Rosa bustled about the new place, cleaning and tending in her motherly way, creating the welcoming atmosphere that everyone dearly loved. In addition, she was pregnant with their ninth child, and was constantly kept busy with sewing, mending and other household duties.

"Maria, help me mend these, will you?"

"Yes, Mama," said Maria reluctantly. She sat beside her mother, enjoying the slight breeze that came through the window. "Mama?"

"Yes, Maria."

"Must you make our panties out of . . . flour sacks?" She looked down at the material in her hands. Bright letters were scattered over the scratchy stuff in advertisement and such.

Rosa's quick fingers didn't miss a beat as she sewed a line of small, tight stitches. "Yes, I must. This is perfectly good material and completely adequate for such use. I could never dream of wasting it."

"Mama?"

"Yes, Maria?"

"They're all the same. How will you tell which is whose?"

Rosa stopped her sewing. A smile crept onto her face as she spoke, "We don't have a measuring stick for no reason, my dear."

Warm summer days brought a lull in the academic realm, and more girls at home only meant livelier hubbub and cheer. With Grazia nearby, the apartment was filled with constant activity. Neighbors and new—found friends were always popping in to say hello or share gossip and news over baked goods, and the headcount only expanded with each friend the girls brought home.

* * *

"No, I don't want to continue going to school. I want to get a job like Giovanna and Maria." A teenaged Michaelina stood with arms crossed, talking with her parents. School was back in session but Michaelina was not interested.

Her mother pleaded. "Michaelina, just a few more years, dear. Giovanna and Maria both went longer than this before they started working."

"I don't care. I'm not Giovanna or Maria, if you hadn't noticed." Michaelina, independent minded like her father, was too stubborn to negotiate. "I don't feel like any more school; I want to get a job now."

"Well too bad," said Raffaele sternly. "Your *madre* says no, and so do I. Stay along in school and then you can get a job in a few years."

"No, I'm not asking for your permission, I'm telling you that I'm getting a job."

*   *Grande (grahn'de):* big, large

CHAPTER TWENTY-EIGHT

Home . . . Right Where It's Always Been

The months passed, and Michaelina got her job.

"I'm sick and tired of watching Papa try to pull in enough money to keep the eight of us, with another one on the way, fed, clothed, educated and cared for," said Michaelina to a friend. She crossed her arms again as she mimicked, "All I ever hear around home is 'Start the fire before you leave for school,' 'Chop some wood and fill the fire box before you go and play,' 'Weed the garden . . .'"

Michaelina sighed. "Well, this is the street where I work," she said as she waved her hand through the air. The girls parted and Michaelina called over her shoulder, "I'll see you tomorrow."

Michaelina worked long and hard hours at G. Fox's Department Store as a bundle girl in the cosmetics department. She proudly earned an average of three dollars and fifty cents a week, which she reluctantly handed over to her father. From her pay, Michaelina was allowed a fifty cents allowance. Giovanna and Maria received an allowance, too, and the girls were free to spend it any way they wished.

"Michaelina," called Raffaele one evening as she arrived home from work.

"Yes, Papa?"

Raffaele motioned with his hand. "Come and sit down, I want to talk to you." Michaelina did as she was told. "What do you think you're doing with all that stuff on your face lately?" Raffaele asked.

Michaelina shrugged. "Just wearing some make-up, Papa. What's wrong with that, huh? All the girls are wearing make-up."

"Not any of my girls," Raffaele said sternly. "I don't like it, Michaelina. Go wash it off."

"That's too bad, isn't it? Because I'm going to wear it."

"What about my authority, Michaelina? What about the way things have always been? You don't tell me what to do. You don't tell me who's boss. I'm boss, I'm your *padre*, and I run this house the way I want it run."

But Raffaele's stern reprimands didn't produce much fruit. Time began to tell that she had a completely different personality than her sisters.

"She disobeys me, she doesn't listen, she does her own thing, her own way and in her own time. There's just no working with her," said Raffaele to Rosa. "I just don't know what to do. Grazia, Giovanna, Maria, they all do what I say . . ."

"Perhaps if she didn't have so much freedom to do what she wanted, then things would be better," suggested Rosa. "Take her to the Underwood Typewriter Factory and let her work there. You can keep an eye on her that way."

Their first winter in Hartford passed without much incident, and the arrival of spring meant the arrival of the new baby.

"Ah, ha," Raffaele said with pleasure. "A boy, I got my boy," smiled Raffaele. "After me, we'll name him Raffaele Guiseppe Marone." It was March 16, 1918 and, much to Rosa's pleasure, the immediate world that surrounded young Raffaele was not a crowded three-room apartment. It was a crowded four-room apartment.

One evening a few weeks later, Rosa glanced out the window as she and some of the girls prepared dinner. "My, what on earth does your *padre* have with him?" She laughed as the other girls peered around her through the window. "Ah, I know what it is." Raffaele had nearly reached the apartment house by now, giving his family a closer look.

"A baby carriage," sang the girls in unison.

* * *

"Michaelina, dear, I'm going for a little walk, and I want you to come." Rosa beckoned to her daughter and the two stepped out of their apartment. "You children, be good, we'll be back soon," Rosa called back over her shoulder.

"Yes, Mama," came the young and simultaneous replies.

"Michaelina, I discovered something last night," explained Rosa as they walked. "You'll never guess what I've found, and I would never have guessed it either, but . . ." Rosa stopped talking as they puffed up a small incline. When she finished her sentence, it was to say, " . . . your *padre* has secured a new house for us."

"Oh," said Michaelina, who then grew silent for a minute. Perhaps she wondered just how many more times their family was going to move. Already, they had lived in three different houses in the last few years. "Well," she finally said, "do you consider this good news or bad news? I mean, if it's bigger than the apartment that would at least be a plus." They walked a little farther before Rosa answered. She was scanning the houses that they were passing.

"I don't know if moving to the house he's chosen will be a good thing or not. That's what this little walk is all about." Rosa laughed. "I want to see what kind of house he just put a fifty-dollar down payment on."

"Fifty dollars," cried Michaelina, then her eyes grew big as she said, "Well, I guess he certainly hasn't been playing with that money we've been earning." They walked up and down the street a couple of times before Rosa stopped with satisfaction. Michaelina noticed a street sign nearby that proclaimed the junction of Hillside Avenue and Ward Place, and a number plaque on a nearby house that read 81.

"Here we are. I'm pretty sure this is the one," confirmed Rosa with a nod. The two stood on the street corner, looking at a big two-story house. Conveniently located, it was across the street from the Wilson Street School, which the Marone girls attended, and a block away from the little local church. There was a veranda off the front of the house, several windows, and a few interesting sights on the other side of the fence that encircled the property.

"A cow pasturing here," laughed Michaelina, "and goats. Mama, it looks a little bit like Laurenzana."

"Well dear," sighed Rosa reluctantly, "I think this is the closest we'll ever get to returning to Laurenzana." She shook her head as if to complain further, but refrained. Instead, she mentioned the size. "*Grande!* It looks good from the outside, and it definitely has more room than the apartment. There's room in the yard for a garden, and even a big shade tree." She turned to Michaelina. "Michaelina, I think this move is going to be a good thing."

Michaelina nodded her agreement.

"And I think it just might be worth the fifty-dollar deposit that your *padre* placed on it."

A few weeks later, Rosa stood in an empty apartment, her hands on her hips. The children had gone ahead with Raffaele to the new house and she took a last look around. Noticing a window she had forgotten to clean, Rosa crossed the room with cleaning cloth in hand. As she wiped off the last of the fingerprints and smudges, she paused. Pleasant sounds and sights were all around, and she closed her eyes with a sigh. The moment she did so, it was as if her entire life passed before her.

She could hear voices, and feel pains and joys all over again. Her happy childhood spent with her brother and parents, her marriage to Raffaele, their children, their home in the rolling hills of Laurenzana, familiar faces of family and friends. For a moment, Rosa stood with her head against the cool glass of the window, contemplating the vivid portrayal that had just taken place of all she had ever felt, dreamed and lived for. As she glanced out the window, Rosa knew that it was all over now. They were settling down and their children were marrying and settling, too.

A tear might well have escaped from her eye and crept down her cheek as a smile slid easily across her face. The world she had been destined to love and enjoy was, as it had always been, right before her very eyes. Raffaele was her family, the love of her life, and the dream she could not smother.

EPILOGUE

The house on Ward Place proved to be the perfect location for the Marones. Gone were the days of living in a cramped apartment, or welcoming child after child. A new life had begun, and the years that followed were filled with family, joy and laughter.

The Marones made constant use of the earth that surrounded their new home, vegetables and small animals populating much of the grounds. Whether it was the popular Italian spirit of frugality or their deep desire to keep traditions of the old country alive and well, we'll never know. Whatever the case, Raffaele kept his wife and daughters busy with potato crops, rabbits, chickens and the like.

The Marone girls were kept busy with school and chores, though Rosa and Raffaele provided a healthy balance of fun. When the "Tooth Fairy" came, the girls received a quarter to spend as they wished. When Santa Claus came, stockings were hung by the stove in the kitchen, filled on Christmas morning with oranges, walnuts, figs, candy and money. The Easter Bunny would bring chocolate eggs and chocolate bunnies, and Rosa's meticulous culinary skills formed dough baskets to hold hard-boiled eggs. She and the girls made mountains of delicious foods, including green soup, sausage pie and ricotta pie for the occasion as well.

On Halloween, the girls would dress up in handmade costumes and enjoy the games and treats that they looked forward to each year, shared, once again, with family and friends. Raffaele often worried that the decorative fence that encircled his property might be knocked down and burned on Halloween and he often spent Halloween night standing guard against troublemakers.

The Fourth of July was perhaps the biggest celebration at the Marones' house, when Raffaele would make batches of homemade ice cream, when sweet watermelons were sliced and eaten by everyone. It was a time when the whole family would walk up the street to Pope Park to watch the big fireworks display, bringing lawn chairs or blankets to sit on. Before the display, there were band concerts to enjoy, and the eventful day would end in cheer.

On Labor Day, the family would ride the trolley to the Charter Oak Fair, in Hartford, where there were rides, petting zoos, horse races and so much more.

The girls frequently visited the Lincoln Dairy Ice Cream Bar, where they hung out with friends and enjoyed a cool treat. A lazy summer afternoon and 15 cents saw the girls going to the movies, while 5 cents could buy them candy. Roller skating, sledding, building snowmen, ice skating, playing checkers and card games entertained the girls, and many an evening would find the family gathered around the radio.

One of Michaelina and Donatine's responsibilities was to take the monthly mortgage payment to Mrs. Harbison. Michaelina and Donatine loved the fifteen-minute walk to Mrs. Harbison's house, where her son would generously offer a slice of apple to the girls, and where her daughter played a beautiful harp. To be in the very presence of such a beautiful instrument was a splendid experience.

When Donatine turned fourteen, Rosa sent her to work along with the other girls, but not without a corset first. Down at the corset shop, Donatine had one fitted before she was allowed to get her first job.

As each daughter grew older and the Marones' income continued to grow, their new house was filled with more furniture. The initial cabinets, chairs, tables and beds, which had often been filled with several girls at once, were soon added to or replaced. The passing years welcomed a radio, pianola, Victrola and more.

The passing of time also brought higher education for the girls. From the Wilson Street School the girls who chose to do so attended the Hartford High School, to which they walked six miles every day. Ella, selectively, chose to go even higher than high school, and attended the Hartford Secretarial School, where she earned the necessary knowledge she later used as an admitting clerk at the Hartford Hospital.

One day, when Ella was young, she and her classmates were in a basic cooking class. In the course of the class, the teacher called on Ella to open one of the large windows. Obediently crossing the room to get the long rod with which she was expected to open the window, Ella began her task. To everyone's surprise, Ella accidentally stuck the rod *through* the window glass. Fresh air was nonetheless obtained.

After the girls had mopped the floors, washed the windows, pulled weeds, washed dishes and tended the youngsters, many an evening would find them, beyond their father's knowledge, in the arms of a male acquaintance twirling around and around to beautiful music. The girls loved to dance, and they did whatever was necessary to provide themselves with that treat. Sometimes that meant lying.

One particular evening, when Michaelina and Donatine were "going over to a friend's house," Raffaele detected that something was amiss and decided to follow them. As they walked down the street to the dance hall, one of the girls turned around only to see Raffaele on their trail! They shrieked. "We're really gonna get it now." But fortunate for them, a car suddenly passed between them and Raffaele, causing him to lose their trail.

Once at the hall, the incident was quickly forgotten as the music started. Michaelina's vigorous dancing, however, often drove her sisters to embarrassment as her high kicks displayed the brightly lettered flour-sack panties. The 10 P.M. curfew would often pass without their notice, and the girls would arrive home well beyond their bedtime.

But fortunate for the girls, Rosa had a number of tactics to keep her husband from hearing them arrive late. She'd leave the door unlocked or ajar, turn the clocks back, keep Raffaele distracted, shoo the girls up to bed and warn that they pull the covers up to their chins. And quickly they must because, while Raffaele never openly expressed his love towards his children, he had a habit of peeking in on each of them after they'd closed their eyes in sleep.

Confident that they were not conscious of his presence, Raffaele stood by their bedsides, for several minutes sometimes, gently kissing their soft foreheads and taking in their innocent features. The girls were often still in their clothes when Raffaele entered their rooms and many times they had to pretend they were sleeping. Sometimes their undershirts were still wet from dancing.

In 1917, the Marone family began to grow once again. This time, however, Rosa and Raffaele sat back as Grazia and Rocco proudly presented Carmella Rizzo. To everyone's dismay, Carmella's young life lasted only a few days. A set of twins were soon to follow, though John and Paul soon joined their sister in the grave.

February 17, 1919 however, brought another Carmella Rose Rizzo into the world, and Rosa and Raffaele were overjoyed. They later received two more grandchildren, as Michael John Rizzo came on May 26, 1924 and Rosanne Grace Rizzo on March 5, 1933.

Giovanna was soon swept off her feet by Paul Mazzarella, who, with Raffaele's permission, of course, married Giovanna in 1920. They settled nearby in a house on Blue Hills Avenue. Francisco John Mazzarella was born on November 4, 1921 and Rose Mazzarella was born in 1922, but died a year later. Two more boys were soon to follow, as Raffaele Paul was born on August 6, 1923 and Paul Frank was born on November 28, 1928.

Maria and Urbano Maccarone married on the 23rd of April 1923. Urbano had immigrated from the town of Bucchianico in the province of Abruzzi, Italy years before. After their marriage, Urbano and his wife settled in a house on Bonnor Street, which was two blocks away from the junction of Ward Place and Hillside Avenue. Maria and Urbano had three sons: Ralph Urban born on May 25, 1925; Justin Salvatore on March 1, 1928 and Armand Anthony on August 11, 1933.

James Lehan crossed paths with Michaelina, and married her on April 17, 1927. James had a dog named James, and whenever a friend called out to him, James' dog would come running. To solve this dilemma, everyone called Michaelina's husband Edward, Ed for short. Michaelina and Ed had two children, a son whom they named Edward Anthony (born on June 13, 1928) and a daughter whom they named Lorraine Antoinette (born on June 13, 1930). The foursome lived on Newington Road, in West Hartford.

On September 5, 1927, Donatine Marone married Michael Battalino. Contrary to the Italian custom of a house-held service and reception, their marriage celebration was hosted in a hall according to Michael's family's wish. Michael and Donatine had three children: Amelia Theresa was born on June 18, 1929; Michael Anthony was born on May 8, 1933 and Donald Carmen was born on May 23, 1939. The Battalinos spent the first two years following their marriage at Ward Place.

When Amelia was young, Raffaele would boost her onto his lap and feed her by hand. Feeding her, that is, with bread crusts dipped in wine. Later, Michael and Donatine moved their small family to 71 Arnold Street, Hartford, where they rented the third floor of Rocco Rizzo's apartment building.

Anna Marone married John Bredice on November 5, 1934. The backyard of the Marone house on Ward Place was filled with furniture as the reception was shared by family and friends. When no one was looking, Amelia approached the kitchen table that now stood in the grass and began to dance atop it, her young heart as light as ever.

Anna and John's first and only child, whom they named Johanna Frances Bredice, arrived on March 4, 1943. When John enlisted for army service in World War II, Anna and Johanna remained at Ward Place, and didn't move into their own home at 59 Tyler Street, Bloomfield, until John returned from the war. Antonetta remained at Ward Place with her sister and niece, until she moved to Bloomfield with the Bredices.

Raffaele Jr. married Frances Cunningham on September 5, 1936. Their first child, whom they named Catherine Agnes, was born on July 16, 1937. A son, Raffaele Joseph, was born on September 16, 1945 and Mary Frances was born on August 19, 1952.

Crowds were always gathered at the Marones' home, be they family, friends, neighbors, or relatives visiting from Italy. Some sort of food was always being prepared or eaten, and the women and girls could be found in the kitchen most of the time. During the fall, while the men and boys were making wine down in the basement, the women and girls would be making sausage, canning vegetables or simply preparing the next meal. The potent smells filled the entire house and escaped out the windows.

Christmas Eve found the entire family gathered at Ward Place, enjoying the fruits of their hard work. Wines, pastas, bread, vegetables and cheeses decked tables and filled stomachs as the adults enjoyed dancing to music from the pianola while the grandchildren fought over whose turn it was to pump it. Amelia, Paul, Ralph and Frank created a music band and the quartet entertained the entire family on many occasions. Gifts would be exchanged, and on Christmas day the family would go to church, later returning to their individual homes to enjoy Christmas dinner.

With the grammar school directly across the street, Rosa saw her grandchildren often, and it was a bad day when no one popped in to say hello or drop in for conversation. Rosa was always waiting with a treat, a hug, a listening ear, a compassionate touch. Family and friends were not the only recipients of her kindness, as Rosa always made extra batches of everything, sending her daughters down the street with a platter of pastries for new and old acquaintances alike.

The completion of a chore was only an excuse for Rosa to send one of the grandchildren to the candy store. Instead of giving them money, Rosa would send them off with an empty bottle, which they could return for two cents to buy a treat. One day, Armand returned to the house with the bottle still in his hand and sadly announced that Mrs. Cohen, the candy store owner, had refused to accept the bottle.

"She said it didn't come from her store."

"Well, we'll see about that," said Rosa, marching young Armand back to the store. Once there, Rosa demanded that her grandchild be given the two cents that he deserved, then stood back with satisfaction as Armand chose his candy.

Rosa, "Mama Non" to the grandchildren, loved to play checkers and would frequently while away the hours with Rosanne, Michael and Armand. Sitting on the cast iron radiator that was adjacent to the kitchen table, Rosa would teach the art of the game to her grandchildren, sneaking an intentional loss so that one of the youngsters could win.

The grandchildren simply loved Mama Non and felt safe and comfortable in her presence. Her house was a place of fun, where little girls could stand above the heat vents and watch their dresses fill up with air, where adventure-some rascals could slide down the banister (which annoyed Antonetta to the point of pinching her little nieces and nephews), run and play games or sit and enjoy each other's company. Rosa always kept a constant supply of pastries around the house, which she encouraged everyone to devour to their heart's content.

The Lincoln Dairy Ice Cream Bar, three buildings down from the Marones' home, was a constant place of interest. The home at Ward Place was a hang-out for friends and family, especially on Sundays, and was always filled with laughter, music, fun and food. Once, before returning home to Italy, Michele Marone bought the entire family ice cream, and the grandchildren got to walk down to the dairy and pay for the cones, then carry the cartons back to the house for everyone to enjoy.

The sound of a delivery truck would drive the children to the windows, where they could see the dust-covered delivery man who always waved a friendly hello. The children watched as he used bags to carry the coal from the back of his truck to the hatchway at the back of the house. The opened hatchway made a certain chute accessible, through which the coal was dumped down. At the bottom of the chute in the basement was a big bin that stored the coal until the furnace needed to be refilled. The basement also housed the garden tools, ash buckets and the like, which the Marones used often.

Life on Ward Place offered the Marones a wide variety of acquaintances, with neighbors' nationalities ranging from Scottish to Irish to Scandinavian. The grandchildren liked to crawl under the fence at the edge of the property and play with the neighbors' children on the other side. Many an afternoon also found them occupying themselves in the closed-in porch or out back on the stone square, which had stone seats around it.

Donald Carmen Battalino was the last grandchild that Raffaele Marone got to see before his death on August 31, 1941. His last days found his mind a little loose and his children, though they were well into their forties, were able to embrace and cuddle him for the first time without his objection.

On November 30, 1948, Rosa also bade her family farewell. Though she missed Ella's wedding by only a few months, Rosa had known Guido Piacentini for quite sometime. Guido was originally from Springfield, Massachusetts, and had met Ella when he came to Connecticut via a job change. Consequently, Guido came to work at the Magovern Company, the same address at which Ella was then working for Murray Memorials.

Ella and Guido were married on Easter Monday, April 18, 1949, at the Hedges in New Britian, Connecticut. Though it was raining outside, the one hundred eighty guests enjoyed the lively occasion with a large buffet and organ music to dance to. Ella had rented an organ for the event, and Amelia lent her talents to provide the wedding march. The service was in the evening and was lit by candles before a fireplace.

Their honeymoon took them to Washington, D.C., where they enjoyed the sites and events of the Capitol. They also visited New York, where memories of her early childhood no doubt returned to Ella's mind. Back in Hartford, the newlyweds remained at Ward Place for the first six months of their marriage, after which Ella took it upon herself to sell the Marone home. They later moved to Agawam, Massachusetts, where they bought a ranch-type house. It was here that Ella gave birth to their first child, Christine Rose Rita Piacentini. She was born on July 1, 1950. In 1952, Ella miscarried a son, whom they had named Richard.

The sale of the house, with the additional money received from selling the stove and pianola, came to $9,255.49. Ella and Antonetta each took a healthy sum for themselves and divided the remaining $8,039 equally among the other seven children.

Rosa and Raffaele's belongings were also dispersed among the children and their families. Kitchenware, clothing, linens and nicknacks began to add touches of the old country to each home. It was the part of Raffaele and Rosa that would keep living, and the part of Italy that would forever remain in the heart of every descending Marone.

HISTORICAL INFORMATION

The AG Vulcan Iron Works in Stettin, Germany, built the *Prinzess Irene* for the North German Lloyd Liner Company in 1900. The liner weighed 10,881 tons, had a width of 60.2 feet, and a length of 523.5 feet. She had a straight bow, two funnels, two masts, two propellers and eight quadruple engines that gave her a maximum speed of fourteen knots. She was constructed with every modern shipbuilding device, with the handling of luggage and the safety and comfort of her passengers in mind. Her main saloon could seat 165 persons.

On June 19, 1900, the *Prinzess Irene* was launched for the Far East service as a new and completed liner. On September 9, 1900, the *Prinzess Irene* made her maiden voyage from Bremen (Northwestern Germany) to Southampton (Southern England), Cherbourg (Northwestern France), New York (USA) and back to Bremen. A little over a month later, the *Prinzess Irene* began a series of seven voyages between Bremen, Suez Canal and the Far East.

April 30, 1903 found the *Prinzess Irene* commencing a new route between Genoa (Northern Italy), Naples (Central Italy) and New York (USA). In 1904, the *Prinzess Irene* ran across a sinking Austrian brigantine, saving its crew of eight men. Early in January of 1907, the *Prinzess Irene* was caught in a strong windstorm on her way to New York. But she was too damaged to continue forward, and Captain Peterssen had no choice but to return her to Italy. Perhaps it was the uncanny return that caused further damage not long after, when the *Prinzess Irene* collided with the *Moltke*. Both were damaged severely and underwent three weeks of repairs. In June of 1909, the *Prinzess Irene* ran across the Cunard Liner *Slavonia*, which had gone ashore on the rocky coast of the Azores. Captain

Peterssen had received the *Slavonia*'s cry for help on his wireless telegraph, and he pulled his liner aside to rescue the *Slavonia*'s crew and three hundred passengers. This rescue took place during adverse weather conditions and was remembered for many years among seamen as a remarkable feat.

January, 1910 found the *Prinzess Irene* in bad weather once again, this time taking her rudder. Captain Peterssen's skill in using the propellers to steer allowed the liner to safely reach her port in Bremen.

During another voyage in February of 1911, the *Prinzess Irene* faced stormy weather and lost a propeller blade while passing through the Strait of Gibraltar. She had to run at a reduced speed until she pulled out of the storm, which at times had winds up to seventy-five miles an hour. The passengers were not allowed to come above deck, and at one point the waves swept aboard, crashing against the *Irene*'s forward deckhouse, breaking rails and tearing away a companion ladder that stood between the steerage and promenade deck. After all this, Captain Peterssen reached New York only one day late.

The voyages from Genoa, Naples and New York continued for eight years, until the *Prinzess Irene* was stranded off Long Island, New York, on April 6, 1911. After being refloated and repaired at Newport News, the *Prinzess Irene* made her final voyage between Genoa, Naples and New York on July 9, 1914. She arrived in New York on the 22nd of the same month, and enjoyed a momentary rest.

The *Prinzess Irene*'s fastest voyage to New York was made when Captain Peterssen agreed to race against the tariff that was in effect at that time. Captain Peterssen managed to arrive with his $1,000,000 cargo of Italian wines within only a few hours of the deadline.

Three years later in April 1917, the United States of America seized the liner for four years, giving her the new name of *Pocahontas*. Speculation has it that the United States government used the liner as a troopship, or another such military related use. In 1921, she was chartered to the United States Mail Steamship Company where she commenced two voyages between New York, Naples and Genoa.

The *Pocahontas* was refitted on February 26, 1921 to accommodate more passengers. Her previous accommodations were 240 first class; 162 second class and 1,954 third class. Adjustments were made to hold 350 cabin, and 900 third-class passengers.

A few months later, the *Pocahontas* commenced her third voyage between America and Italy on May 22. But, the *Pocahontas* only made it as far as the Strait of Gibraltar, where she was laid up with machinery defects. It was a year later before the North German Lloyd Line bought her back and towed her to Germany. There she was reconditioned and, once again, renamed.

On April 7, 1923, she began sailing under the name of *Bremen* between Bremen (Northwestern Germany) and New York. Three years later, the *Bremen* was refitted once again, this time to carry cabin, tourist third cabin, and third-class passengers.

On September 28, 1927, the *Bremen* commenced her last voyage from Bremen, Cobh (Southern Republic of Ireland) to New York, where she was renamed in 1928 as the *Karlsruhe*. By changing her name, the *Karlsruhe* allowed her previous name to be used for a newly constructed express liner.

The *Karlsruhe* commenced her first voyage on January 29, 1928, sailing from Bremen to Cobh and New York. Later, the *Karlsruhe* sailed from Bremen to Boulogne (Northern France), Galway, (Western Republic of Ireland), Halifax, New York, Havana (Northwestern Cuba), Vera Cruz (Gulf of Mexico) and Tampico (Eastern Mexico). This was definitely her longest voyage, which was commenced on August 16, 1931.

In June of 1932, the *Karlsruhe* started a new route from Bremen, Halifax and Galveston (South Eastern Texas). This new route continued until August 20, when the *Karlsruhe* commenced her last Bremen—Halifax—Galveston voyage. From Galveston, she sailed to Bremen, where she was retired and scrapped later that year.

FAMILY TREE

Donato and Maria Giovanna Pavese—Michele, Rosa
Antonio and Graziado Marone—Maria Carmella, Raffaele

•

Raffaele and Rosa Marone—Grazia, Giovanna, Maria, still born son, Michaelina, Donatine, Antonio, Rocchitella, Anna, Antonetta, Raffaele

•

Grazia and Rocco Rizzo—Carmella, John and Paul, Carmella, Michael, Rosanne
Giovanna and Paul Mazzarella—Frank, Rose, Ralph, Paul
Maria and Urbano Maccarone—Ralph, Justin, Armand
Michaelina and Edward Lehan—Edward Jr., Lorraine
Donatine and Michael Battalino—Amelia, Donald, Michael
Rocchitella and Guido Piacentini—Christine, Richard
Anna and John Bredice—Johanna
Antonetta
Raffaele Marone and Frances Cunningham—Catherine, Ralph, Mary Frances

Chronology

1867—February 15, Raffaele born to Antonio and Graziado Marone
1879—March 2, Rosa born to Donato and Maria Giovanna Pavese
1880—Rosa is kidnapped as a baby
    Maria Giovanna returns to Italy with Michele and Rosa
1884—Raffaele makes first trip to America and gets a job
1885—Raffaele becomes an American citizen
1886 through 1910—Raffaele travels between Italy and America
1896—January 6, Raffaele Marone marries Rosa Pavese (date speculatory)
1897—March 6, Grazia Marone born
1899—November 16, Giovanna Marone born
1902—February 26, Maria Carmella Marone born
    Rosa diagnosed with smallpox
1903—still born son delivered
1904—October 6, Michaelina Rosa Morone born
1906—July 6, Donatine Maria Marone born
1911—March 27, Marones leave for America
    April 6, North German Lloyd liner *Prinzess Irene* ran aground off Fire Island, Long Island, NY
    April 9, passengers transferred from stranded liner and arrive on Ellis Island, New York
    July 26, Antonio Marone born
1913—January 9, Rocchitella Rita Marone born
    May 7, Antonio Marone dies
1914—September 14, Anna Rosa Marone born
1916—March 14, Antonetta Marie Marone born
    April 16, Grazia Marone marries Rocco Rizzo
    Rocco and Grazia move to Hartford, Connecticut
1917—Marones move to Hartford, Connecticut
    Carmella Rizzo born
    Carmella Rizzo dies (ten days old)
1918—March 16, Raffaele Guiseppe Marone born
    John and Paul Rizzo born (year speculatory)
    John and Paul Rizzo die (three days old)

1919—February 17, Carmella Rosa Rizzo born
1920—Giovanna Marone marries Paul Mazzarella (year speculatory)
1921—November 4, Francisco John Mazzarella born
1922—Rose Mazzarella born
1923—April 23, Maria Carmella Marone marries Urbano Maccarone
      August 6, Raffaele Paul Mazzarella born
      Rosa and Ella take train trip back to New York
      Rose Mazzarella dies
1924—May 26, Michael John Rizzo born
1925—May 25, Ralph Urban Maccarone born
1927—April 17, Michaelina Rosa Marone marries Edward Lehan
      September 5, Donatine Maria Marone marries Michael Battalino
1928—March 1, Justin Salvatore Maccarone born
      June 13, Edward Anthony Lehan, Jr. born
      November 28, Paul Frank Mazzarella born
      Ella gets first job as sales clerk at S & A Five and Ten Cent Store
1929—June 18, Amelia Theresa Battalino born
      Ella takes first airplane ride
      Ella gets first office job, working at the Connecticut Home Supply
1930—June 13, Lorraine Antoinette Lehan born
1933—March 5, Rosanne Grace Rizzo born
      May 8, Michael Anthony Battalino born
      August 11, Armand Anthony Maccarone born
1934—November 5, Anna Rosa Marone marries John Bredice
1936—September 5, Raffaele Guiseppe Marone marries Frances Cunningham
1937—July 16, Catherine Agnes Marone born
1939—May 23, Donald Carmen Battalino born
1941—August 31, Raffaele Marone dies
1943—March 4, Johanna Frances Bredice born
1945—September 16, Ralph Joseph Marone born
1948—November 30, Rosa Pavese Marone dies

1949—April 18, Ella Rita Marone marries Guido Piacentini
    October, Ella sells the house on Ward Place
1950—July 1, Christine Rose Rita Piacentini born
1952—August 19, Mary Frances Marone born
    Richard Piacentini miscarried
1973—April 10, Guido Piacentini dies
1979—January 6, Giovanna Marone Mazzarella dies
1980—December 27, Grazia Marone Rizzo dies
1982—June 16, Michael Anthony Battalino dies
1987—June 15, Maria Carmella Marone Maccarone dies
1992—May 4, Raffaele Guiseppe Marone dies
1994—August 15, Donatine Maria Marone Battalino dies
1999—June 22, John Bredice dies
2002—December 24, Rocchitella Rita Marone Piacentini dies

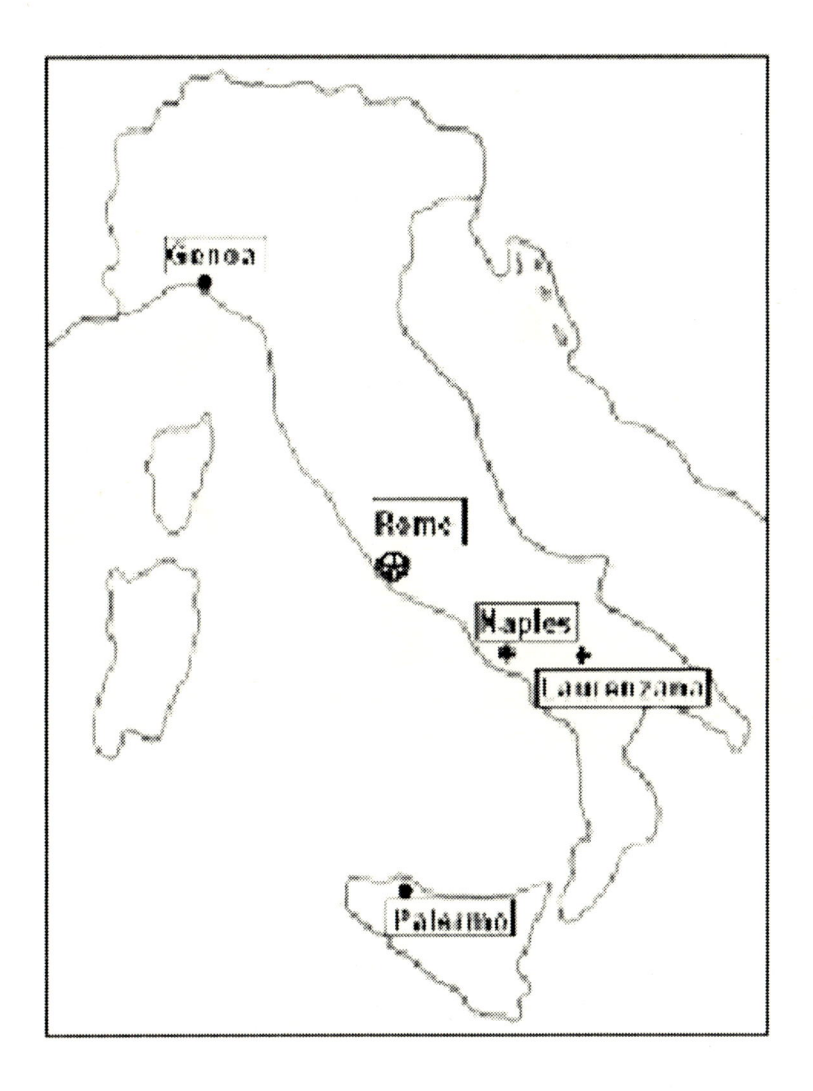

Location of Laurenzana, Italy.

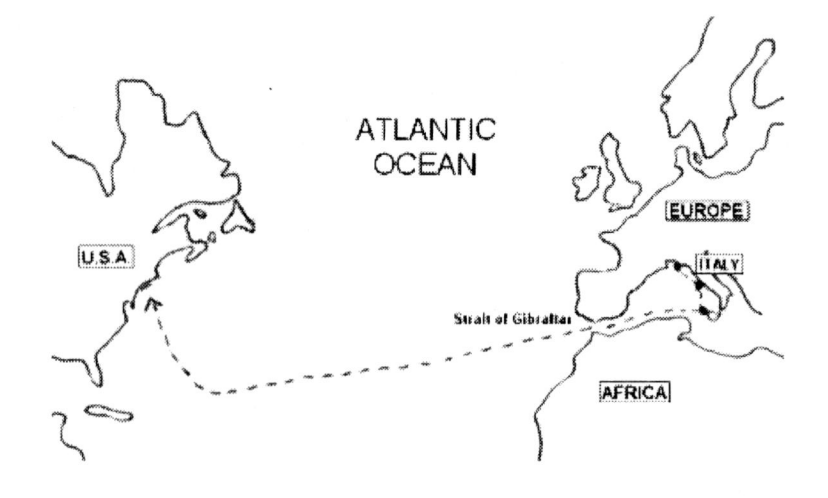

Route of the *Prinzess Irene* from Genoa, Naples, Palermo, Gibraltar to New York.

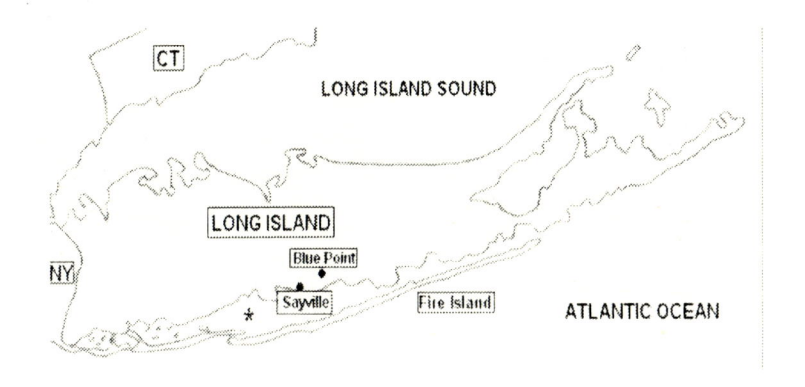

Approximate locations of Sayville and
Blue Point in relation to Fire Island.

*   Great South Bay

Friday, April 7, 1911. Lifesavers battle vicious waves in their attempt to reach the *Prinzess Irene.* Photo courtesy of The New York Times Agency.

Sunday, April 9, 1911. Lifesavers observe the stranded *Prinzess Irene* amid their lifeboats from the shore of Fire Island. Photo courtesy of The New York Times Agency.

Captain Frederic von Letten Peterssen of the *Prinzess Irene* (right) and Captain Prehn of the *Prinz Friedric Wilhelm* (left). Photos courtesy of The New York Times Agency.

1913. The Marones have their picture taken for the first time. Back from L to R: Grazia, Giovanna. Front from L to R: Michaelina, Maria, Rosa (sitting), Raffaele (holding Ella) and Donatine. Photo courtesy of Ella Piacentini.

1930's. The Marones gather for another family picture. Standing from L to R: Anna, Ella, Donatine, Grazia, Giovanna, Maria and Michaelina. Sitting from L to R: Raffaele Jr., Raffaele, Rosa and Antonetta.
Photo courtesy of Ella Piacentini.

The four remaining Marones (at the time of this writing). Clockwise from top left: Antonetta, Ella, Michaelina, Anna. Photo courtesy of Gary Carra.

Donato and Maria Giovanna Pavese.
Photos courtesy of Ella Piacentini.

The Marones' home at 81 Ward Place, Hartford,
Connecticut. Photo courtesy of Antoinette Marone.

AUTHOR'S NOTE

The information in the pages you have just read has been thoroughly researched and taken only from reliable sources. All available dates and details (major and minor) have been included. All information included in the introduction has been documented according to the memories that immediate Marone members shared. Descriptions of the house in Laurenzana, the scenario of hired help, wheat fields, livestock and harvest celebrations are also documented accordingly.

The events surrounding the grounding of the North German Lloyd liner *Prinzess Irene* are historically accurate and have been recorded in this book as found in the April 6, 7, 8, 9, 10, and 11, 1911 editions of *The New York Times* newspaper. The grounding and rescue details found in chapters eleven through eighteen were taken directly from *The New York Times* newspaper articles mentioned above. The information in chapters seventeen and eighteen was taken word for word from *The New York Times* newspaper.

All articles from *The New York Times* newspaper were obtained from microfilm at the Hartford Public Library, Hartford Connecticut. All information taken from *The New York Times* newspaper was used by permission from The New York Times Agency.

The location and descriptions of the tenement apartment and the house on the corner of Ward Place and Hillside Avenue are true to Marone individuals' memories. The house on the corner of Hillside Avenue and Ward Place still stands today in Hartford, Connecticut.

During the time the Marones occupied it, the house had a total of seven rooms, complete with kitchen, dining room, living room, bedrooms, and a small attic space for ventilation, accessible by trap door. There was a full basement, accessible by a set of interior stairs, as well as a hatchway out the back of the house. The basement held the furnace, but was also used for making and storing wine.

The Maccarones' own basement, on Bonnor Street two blocks up from Ward Place, was much too small for making wine so each year Urbano made wine in the Marones' basement, working with *paesani** to produce an annual amount of one hundred gallons for his own family's use. Wooden cases filled with grapes were delivered to Ward Place each year, and the men would carry their prized boxes down through the hatchway to the large area beneath the house which provided the necessary room to complete all the steps to making the wine. There was a smaller room, partitioned off from the larger room and much cooler than the rest of the basement, which made a perfect storage room complete with wooden casks for the wine.

Through the years, it became Urbano's sons' responsibility to fill the bottles and keep the supply at their home replenished. The wine was stored in two fifty-gallon barrels, which were air tight so that the wine wouldn't turn to vinegar. The small amount of wine that dribbled out of the spigot made filling the wine bottles a slow process. Many a time Maria shooed her boys out the door to refill a bottle before Urbano returned from work or company arrived. Michele Marone used the cellar, too, and stored imported Italian cheese in the cool darkness while wholesale profits were made.

The bedrooms were upstairs and a hallway ran on both floors of the house. A gas light hung on the wall outside each bedroom and the jets would be lit each night. When these were later converted to electricity, the gas jets were used as clothes hangers, everyone hanging their spare sweater or night shirt on the walls.

In later years, Rosa was privileged to have a cast iron stove in her kitchen, which burned coal, and she enjoyed an ice box to keep the food refrigerated. When more revisions were made, a "real" refrigerator and washing machine took the place of the icebox and washboard. Radiators then heated the house with hot water, and screens were put on the windows. Since then, some amount of interior remodeling has most likely taken place.

* *Paesani (pie sahnee):* Italians from the same city/village/town